# Harbor Lights & Broken Hearts

## JENNIFER WALTERS

BARBRA JUNE PUBLISHING

*For my sister, Jacquline Prescott*
*Whose love has been a*
*Constant in every chapter*
*Of my life.*

This is a work of fiction. All of the characters, organizations, businesses, and events portrayed in this novel are either products of the author's imagination or are used fictitiously.

Cover photo design by Kristin Bryant

Author photo taken by April Krompatich at Appletree Photography

# Other Books by Jennifer Walters

The Turtle Creek Series

The Memories We Keep

A Side Lake Summer

Return to Side Lake

Christmas in Side Lake

Take Me to Side Lake


The Admonson's Sisters Series

Harbor Lights & Broken Hearts


The Fredrickson's Series

Always Right Here

Northern Winds

Greenrock Road


Other Books By Jennifer Walters

The Weight of Change

# CHAPTER 1

## *Vivian*

THE PIERCING WAILS woke me up at three in the morning. I plopped my pillow over my head and groaned, hoping it would stop. After what felt like an hour, I finally got up and made my way into my guest room. My sister sat in the rocking chair, my little niece's cries only getting louder.

"What's going on? Why is she crying so hard? This isn't like her."

My sister wiped her already exhausted eyes with the back of her hand and my eyes softened. I hated to see her like this. "Liv, are you okay?"

She shook her head as she put Melody over her shoulder and patted her back. "I'm worried. She's had a fever all night and a horrible cough. Do you think I should take her in?"

I walked closer and held out my arms. "Let me try, okay? I know you haven't had much sleep so let's see if I can calm her down and help bring her fever down. Did you give her Tylenol?"

Melody snuggled into my arms, and I kissed the top of her warm head.

Her bottom lip whimpered as she stared back at me and cried.

"Yes, it should be kicking in by now."

Olivia stood up and stared at Melody in my arms. "You don't have to do this. You just got home. You've hardly had any sleep yourself."

Melody's cries seemed to be getting softer as I swayed her back and forth. "I'm fine, seriously. I can sleep in tomorrow. You can't."

"I guess that's true. I think she likes you more than she likes me. How did you calm her down so quickly?"

"Who knows. Maybe she could tell you were tense. You need some sleep, or you won't be any good to take care of her tomorrow. She needs a healthy mom."

Her eyes lit up. "Thank you so much, Vivian. Please, if her temperature gets any higher come get me. I just need a couple minutes of sleep."

From the dark circles under her eyes, she needed a few days of sleep.

She kissed Melody on the head and disappeared before I had a chance to change my mind. I tried to help her when I could because being a single mom was not easy. She was home most of the time by herself or helping take care of our parents because I was so busy running my bar and playing on my volleyball league. I liked to keep busy to avoid thinking about how lonely I felt.

Melody was just over three months old this February. My sister and I had finally rekindled our relationship and were living together. My heart felt a little less empty, but the crying in the middle of the night had me regretting it at times. I really thought Ben would come back after the baby was born. That he would want to be a part of her life, but he stopped answering Olivia's calls. Even my brother Tim tried to get a hold of him to let him know he was now a father, but he was not responding to anyone. I wanted to hunt down that guy and beat the crap out of him.

Melody was sleeping now, so I put her pacifier in her

mouth and set her down in her bassinet, careful not to wake her. I hummed and rubbed her tummy gently before touching her forehead with the back of my hand. Her forehead was no longer so hot. Perhaps the fever had finally broke.

I crawled back into bed and pulled the blankets over my head. I was unable to warm up this time of year. I was chilled all the time. I loved Minnesota, but below zero was just too damn cold.

I finally dragged myself out of bed at noon. Olivia and Melody were already gone. I knew Liv wanted to get out of the house so I could sleep. She was so thoughtful like that. She probably took Melody over to our parents' house on the east side of Duluth or they went grocery shopping. I opened up the fridge, but I could not find anything to eat. I shut the door again. Hopefully they went grocery shopping but most likely they were at my parents house.


By the time I cleaned up the house, did laundry, and baked my homemade banana bread, it was already quarter to five. My mother hated it when I was late for dinner. We had dinner at my parents every Sunday night. It had always been that way. Dinner used to include all my siblings, but they all moved away, and we had some family issues long ago that had most of us still feuding and holding long grudges. My parents hated it. We were always so close growing up.

Olivia had been at our parents' house all day helping our mother make dinner, after all. Our parents were both having health problems, and Olivia spent a lot of time there, caring for them until she went back to work. We were talking about hiring a nurse around the clock so they could stay out of a nursing home. Our childhood home was way too big for our parents to upkeep, and it was too big for just the two of them. Olivia and I both tried talking to them about selling it and buying a smaller place, but they would not consider it. The house held too many memories, and they refused to sell, but eventually they would have to give in.

Tim and Lizzy were the first two faces I saw when I walked in. Although I had only met Lizzy a handful of times, I could tell how happy my brother was with her. "You guys came all this way for Sunday dinner, huh?" I said, hugging them both.

"We could smell Mom's lasagna from Side Lake," Tim said.

I smiled at Lizzy as she held Melody. "She's just the sweetest little thing and she looks just like her mama. I've missed you. Liv. Side Lake just isn't the same without you. Everyone misses you."

Olivia smiled at her. "I miss you, too. I miss all you guys."

I leaned closer to Tim. "When are you going to have one of those?"

Tim gave me a warning look and turned it back on me. "When are you going to have one of those?"

I laughed. "Probably never. That's what my siblings are for. To have babies so I can be the fun aunt."

Tim raised a brow. "Speaking of. When was the last time you spoke with any of your other sisters? You girls ever going to make up?"

I waved him off. "The phone goes both ways."

"Let her be," Mom said. "Now, how is everything going in Side Lake?"

"Good. I can't wait for the snow to melt and spring to arrive. Winter is so long," Lizzy said.

"Don't let her fool you. She started cross country skiing and snowmobiling with me. She'll be sad when there isn't any snow left."

Lizzy handed Melody to Tim. "Not true. I love summers in Side Lake."

"Me too," Olivia said.

I cleared my throat. "Lizzy, how's your uncle doing?"

Olivia looked my way and rolled her eyes. I knew my question would piss her off, but I also knew she wanted to know the answer. Olivia lived with Tim in Side Lake for a few months and when I went to pick her up and bring her back home, she had a hard time leaving. She had fallen for Lizzy's uncle, Troy. He was a widower, losing his wife to cancer a few years back. He seemed nice enough but in no way did I want my sister to fall for a guy that was emotionally unavailable.

Tim and Lizzy had a close group of friends on Turtle Creek Road in Side Lake, which was a small lake town an hour and a half north of Duluth. My sister got too comfortable there and considered moving there permanently so I had to talk some sense into her and she moved back to help with my parents who were getting older and needed some caretaking. She was living in a fictional world there, the aftermath of a divorce. Her heart was broken and I knew she wasn't thinking clearly.

When she was living in Side Lake all those months I missed her so much. She helped me out with the restaurant when I needed it. When her husband Ben left her and took off to London, abandoning her and their baby, she needed to get away for a while and that's when she went to Side Lake. Tim convinced her to stay for the summer. But home in Duluth was where she belonged. My parents needed her, and I did, too.

Lizzy cleared her throat and looked at Olivia, an uncomfortable expression on her face. "He's doing…good. His store has been extremely busy for the holidays, and he's even starting to read now."

Olivia gave me the side eye, with a warning in her eyes.

I pushed a smile and glanced back at Lizzy. "What kind of books does he read?"

Olivia turned around. "I'm going to rock Melody to sleep."

"Thrillers. A good friend of ours writes romance books so

he even started reading them," Lizzy said. "But how are you doing? Tim said you own a restaurant here, and we've heard the food is unbelievable."

"Yeah, you guys should come in sometime. It's called Zenith Bar and Grill. We have the best burgers around and on Saturday nights we always have a DJ or a band."

She nodded. "That sounds great. What about this weekend?" she said, looking at Tim.

He shrugged. "Works for me. I don't think we have anything going on."

"It's pretty quiet this time of year, but I'll reserve a table for you guys anyway." I was excited to get to know Lizzy better. "Or you can just sit at the bar."

Although my three other sisters and I had not spoken in years, I really missed having sisters around to hang out with. My sisters and I had nothing but conflicts after high school and they escalated to the point where no one spoke anymore. Sure, Olivia and I were close, but we had our issues too. The rest of our sisters stayed far away and never came around for the holidays.

Only my sister Charlee showed up at Olivia's baby shower at my restaurant, I was so busy cooking for the event and running the games, we never had a chance to chat. I was okay with that because speaking to each other after all this time would have been awkward. My mother never gave up on trying to get us all together, but everyone had excuses why they couldn't make it to our parents' house again this year for Christmas. Mom and Dad were heartbroken about it, and I did not blame them.

We all sat around the table for dinner.

Tim cleared his throat and took Lizzy's hand and kissed it. "We have some news for you guys, and we wanted to tell you in person."

I took a sip of wine. My intuition told me they had some big news to tell us, and I had a feeling I knew what it was.

Tim put his arm around Lizzy and they smiled at each other. "We're having a baby."

"Oh!" Mom jumped up and hugged Lizzy, and Dad shook Tim's hand.

"Congratulations," Olivia and I both said.

"There's more."

What else could there be?

"We're having twins," Tim said, so proudly.

"No shit!"

"Language, Vivian," Olivia said, her hands over Melody's ears.

"The damage is done. I don't think plugging her ears now is going to help."

"Vivian," my mom said, a warning tone in her voice.

"What? It's not like she even understands what we're saying anyway."

My mom rolled her eyes at me and shifted her attention to the happy couple. "Congratulations. You're going to make fine parents."

And I was going to be alone for the rest of my life. I stood up to grab a glass of wine but came back with the whole bottle in my hand.

"The glasses are in the cupboard, Viv," Mom said with a warning expression.

"Nah, why dirty a glass?" I took a few loud gulps. Everyone stared at me. I set the bottle down on the table. "What? Did someone else want some?"

# CHAPTER 2

## *Liam*

THE DINNER RUSH WAS OVER. Now came the in between time when anyone over forty went home, and the young twenty and thirty-year-olds would start coming in for appetizers and drink cocktails until the early hours of the morning.

I checked the coolers and made my way to the basement to fill my list. The mildewy air down the stairs had me holding my breath. It took a minute to get used to it. Vivian planned on scrubbing the place down, but she did not have the time. I'd volunteered so many times to do it, but she felt like I already did so much. Little did she know I did not mind; I'd do anything for her. I grabbed three cases of beer and made my way back up to the bar.

The dinner vibe had been replaced with loud music and an assortment of lights. I took two steps before I saw her. Her brown curls and emerald eyes took my breath away. She always complained about her curls in one breath but admitted curls were easier to manage than taking the time to straighten her hair. She was always so busy trying to run this restaurant and bar, going above and beyond to make sure every customer was happy, and every employee well treated.

"You're early and already stocking my coolers. What am I going to do when you decide to leave? Please promise me you aren't planning on leaving anytime soon."

I grinned. "And leave you to run this place all alone? Never in a million years. Plus, I haven't figured out a way to convince you to go on a date with me yet."

She grabbed a case off the counter and squatted down to stock the Hamm's, Minnesota beer. "Oh, Liam. Will you ever stop messing with me? You know I'm already married to this bar. It's the perfect love hate relationship, really."

I was far from giving up on her. I was her bar manager and her right-hand man. An accountant by day during tax season, changing into a bartender by night. She would never want a relationship to get in the way of that. We'd been best friends for years.

She had no clue what she did to me. Every time I saw her, my heart skipped a beat. She was unbelievably gorgeous and kind. She turned every head when she walked into a room with her wit and beauty. Confidence radiated off her, and it was hot.

Vivian walked around the bar then glanced back at me and winked. I held my breath and stared as she walked around the corner and out of view.

"Close your mouth, Liam, I think you're drooling." Alyssa hip checked me, and I bumped her back.

"I don't know what you're talking about."

"Oh, come on. Everyone can see it. The two of you are always flirting and every time you look at Liv you're undressing her with your eyes." She laughed. "Just ask her out already."

I squatted down and ripped open the next case of beer to stock the empty shelf. "I am not. You make me sound like a stalker. She's hot and funny and I like talking to her, okay? But she's my boss."

She squeezed my shoulder. "Okay, keep telling yourself

that." She squatted down next to me and whispered, "Do you know what I think?"

"I don't ever know what you're thinking, Alyssa."

"I think you're scared."

I jumped to my feet. "I'm not scared, I just know the kind of guys she goes for and they definitely aren't me."

She closed the cooler and stood up next to me. "Oh, you mean the ass holes that always cheat on her? It's because she hasn't found the right guy. She's probably just scared to commit. Plus, you're so much hotter than they are." She leaned over the bar as she wiped it down. "For some reason she always goes for the bad boys. You could be the guy to change that. I'm just saying. Get out of that friend zone or you'll never have a chance."

A man yelled above the loud music, "Two Greyhound's, please."

Alyssa grabbed a bottle of vodka, threw it in the air, and caught it as she filled the glass while simultaneously grabbing the grapefruit juice with her other hand and pouring it in the glass.

The man set the money on the table and leaned on the bar with a cocky grin. "Hey baby, you like bacon? Wanna strip?"

Alyssa turned her back to him and put the money in the register. When she turned around he continued to try his luck. "What time do you get off, beautiful? I could show you a good time."

She took one step forward, smiled sweetly, then gave him the middle finger. "Not a chance, buddy."

He laughed and threw his hands in the air. "Okay, playing hard to get I see. You have no idea what you just passed up."

"You tipped me a dollar. I'm pretty sure I do." With that she turned her back and flipped her hair over her shoulder.

Alyssa was gorgeous, and she knew it. She made more tips than pretty much everyone at the bar. She walked with a slightly exaggerated movement that showed her confidence.

She knew exactly how to give men the attention they needed to keep those tips coming, but also how to tell them to get lost when she needed to.

"See, that guy knows how to ask for what he wants. He's confident but a little too cocky. He's the type of jerk women like Vivian gravitate toward for some reason. She needs a Brandon not a Dylan, she just doesn't know it yet."

"A Brandon?" I asked confused.

"Yes, Brandon Walsch. Don't you have any sisters that watched Beverly Hills 90210?"

"How old do you think I am? That was from like the 90's, right?"

She rolled her eyes. "Brandon was the good boy, that's all I'm saying."

"Brandon?" Vivian said, coming around the bar. "Who's Brandon?"

"Liam here doesn't know who Brandon Walsch is."

She shook her head at me and then looked back at Alyssa. "I don't really know what people saw in him. I was more of a Dylan girl with his sexy scar and bad boy ways. Hot."

Alyssa smiled at me with raised eyebrows, proving her point.

"Hey muscles, want to tap another keg? We're running low on Bent Paddle," Vivian shouted over the music that was suddenly so loud we had a hard time talking.

"On it, boss."

When I returned to the bar Vivian was already gone. Alyssa was chatting with a couple of guys at the bar while she poured a line of Jagger Bombs. I could not hear what they were saying, but they were staring at her chest as she moved around the bar to bring them more beers.

I grabbed a pitcher and put it under the spout. It sprayed a bit and then turned to foam before finally coming out a liquid.

"Liam, pineapple juice and cranberry juice," Alyssa said.

"You got it."

I raced to the back fridge, grabbed the juice, but as I passed the kitchen, I heard Vivian's voice. I peeked in to make sure she did not need any help. We'd been down some waiters lately, and I worried she was in panic mode. I looked around the kitchen but could not see her. I heard her voice again, so I walked over to the pantry and turned on the light. There she stood with the phone in her hand and tears in her eyes.

It had to be that guy again. Why did she always pick the worst of them?

"Jimmy, stop calling me. You know I'm working."

I held out my hand for the phone but she shook her head. . Her eyes pleaded with me as she held the phone away from her ear. "I got this. Get back out to the bar, please."

I lifted her chin and swiped my thumb under her eyes. "Are you sure?"

Vivian nodded, her lip quivering.

I wanted to wrap her in my arms and then scream at that jerk, but she would not want me to. Instead, I smiled gently and walked away, turning off the light on my way out.

I got back into bartender mode. I flirted with the women and smiled more than I'd ever admit. The tips were rolling in and Alyssa was a rockstar. Vivian returned soon after and we all scrambled to serve drinks to the full bar.

Vivian was the reason this bar was so successful. She was great with people and made time to greet them all at their tables, to socialize, and ask them about their food. By the end of the night, we'd emptied our tip jar pitcher at least ten times and most of the clients were tipsy. The last person left the bar at two thirty, and I had to walk at least thirty women to their cars.

"What a night. We killed it," Alyssa said, putting on her jacket.

I picked her gloves up from the counter and handed them to her. "Do you want me to walk you out?"

"Nah, my ride is waiting out front." She leaned in to whisper in my ear, "I bet I know someone who may need your assistance though." She raised her eyebrows and nodded her head toward Vivian who had just finished mopping up.

"Get out of here," I said with a laugh and a shake of my head. "You're never going to stop, are you?"

She patted me on the shoulder. "Not a chance."

I followed her to the door and locked it behind her, watching out the window to make sure she got into her boyfriend's car safely. A lot of crazy people were around, so I worried about the women I worked with. Guys could be real idiots when they were drinking.

Vivian was sitting at the bar, paperclipping the money and slipping the clips into a bank bag.

She preferred to take an Uber when she worked late to avoid having to find a parking spot. Sometimes she even walked to work for the exercise. "Do you need a ride?"

She threw my jacket at me. "Actually, that would be great. I was going to call an Uber but I'm too exhausted to wait for it. You don't mind?"

Mind? There was nothing I wanted more. "It's on my way. Why are you so tired? That baby keeping you up again?"

"It just breaks my heart. Liv's so exhausted all the time, and she's such a good mom."

"She's lucky she has you."

"I don't know if I'd go that far."

A strand of hair fell in front of her eye. Without thinking, I tucked it behind her ear. Our eyes locked and we stood there staring at each other, unable to move.

She cleared her throat and stepped to the side. "We should probably go."

"You're right. Let's get out of here."

We were so close to kissing. I wanted to feel her lips on mine. I knew it was a terrible idea, and would complicate everything. I was not her type and I knew that. But I struggled to convince my heart.

# CHAPTER 3

## *Vivian*

I SHUT my front door and peeked out the window at him, careful to hide behind the curtains. Liam was such a tease. His hand was always touching me somewhere. On the ride home, he comforted me by placing his hand on my leg when I told him Jimmy was not giving up on us. His touch gave me shivers when all he was trying to do was be friendly.

Jimmy was a handsome bad boy, my latest flavor of the month. He was mean and rude and a criminal. He had tattoos up his neck, and I'd caught him flexing his chest muscles and kissing his biceps. He was disgusting, really, but also a challenge. He had a terrible upbringing and made impulsive decisions. I had this way of finding men with the most issues and trying to fix them. It took all the spotlight off me, and it made me feel good to help fix them. Not that I ever really fixed them, but I tried. I struggled to stay away, giving him far too many chances and I knew it.

My sisters always said I gravitated toward men that were trouble, and they were right. I never admitted it, but I think it was my way of making sure my relationships did not last.

I was a terrible player and ended up falling in love with them until they did or said such terrible things that I had to walk away. Jimmy was no different. I caught him stealing two bottles of top shelf whisky before I finally had to kick him out of my bar and my life for good.

Liam would have kicked the crap out of Jimmy if he'd known. He hated the men I dated, and he wanted to protect me. He was such a gentleman like that. If only I could fall for a guy like Liam, but I never would. He was not broken enough for me. He was also too good for me.

At home, I heard the sound of sobbing coming from Olivia's room, and not baby sobbing. I listened by her door and heard my sister's muffled sobs. I knocked gently, tapping with my knuckles before opening up the door.

Olivia shot out of bed, rubbing her tears away, and forced a smile my way. Her bedside lamp was on, and she had a book in her hand. I rushed to her side and sat on the bed, wrapping her up in a giant hug. "Are you okay?"

She nodded. "Yeah, just a lot on my mind."

"Do you want to talk about it?"

She seemed to think about it before shaking her head. "It's nothing, probably just a little post partum depression or something."

I rested my hand on her arm. "I know it isn't easy. What Ben did is selfish. I'm so sorry you're going through this."

She shook her head. "It's not him, really. He made the decision to run from our lives and not be around for his daughter, so she's better off without him. It's just a lot. My life went from single nurse to stay at home mom with spit up all over my clothes, and I always smell like puke." She laughed through her tears.

"Don't forget spending all your free time taking care of our parents, which can be a lot. Thank you for that, by the way." I wiped her tears away with my thumb. "Have you spoken to Troy lately?"

"He doesn't want to talk to me. He's busy, you heard

Lizzy. He has a store and a life in Side Lake. He doesn't want to talk to some woman with a baby."

Although I hardly knew Troy, l knew my sister regretted leaving him. He was a grieving widower and she distracted him from that pain. They were not really serious. From what I saw they were just two lonely people who gravitated toward each other.

"How about we talk to Mom and Dad and see if they'll watch Melody tomorrow night? You can come to my restaurant, have a few drinks and enjoy yourself."

"Watching Melody might be too much for them."

"Miss Hanson could come over and help them. They already have the crib. What do you say?"

She looked away for a moment before turning back to me. "If you can get Miss Hanson to help and stay the night, I'll have no choice but to say yes."

"Deal," I said.

Miss Hanson was a pre-school teacher and my parent's next-door neighbor. She was single and wanted children of her own, but she had not met the right guy yet. She was fresh out of college and had been a nanny while at University of Minnesota Duluth. Her mother lived next to us since we were babies and when she passed, Tammy inherited the house. She got a job at the local school, and we all started calling her Miss Hanson. The nickname started from a joke Tim made, and it stuck. She was the perfect person for the job.


Tammy sent a message on Saturday at noon and said she would love to help look after Melody. Olivia seemed almost disappointed when I told her.

"I've never left her overnight before. Maybe I won't be able to stay up that late. I'm used to going to bed at eight o'clock because she wakes up two to three times in the night."

I laughed. "You will have a blast. Alyssa and Liam will take good care of you."

"Who are Alyssa and Liam?"

"My co-workers. You'll love them, trust me." She looked so nervous. "Oh, and Liam's single in case you're wondering."

I lost my breath at the thought of Liam and Olivia hooking up. Why did that make me so jealous? Probably because he was my best friend, and he gives me so much attention. If and when he dated someone, I might not get the playful banter I'm so accustomed to. Yeah, that was the reason. It had to be.

"I'm not looking for a relationship. Definitely not."

I put my hands up in surrender. "Maybe not but it could be a fun distraction."

She rolled her eyes.


Olivia showed up at eight. She sat down at the back bar and ordered a burger and a beer. I expected I would need to convince her to have a drink, but it looked like she was already letting her guard down. Good.

As the night went on, she chatted with both Alyssa and Liam. Once the music started, Liam had to lean in closer to talk to her. I was busy waiting tables and helping train the new waitress, Jillian, who had a case of the dropsies tonight. She had spilled beer on me, a customer, and also dropped a tray of wine glasses after she finished cleaning off the table. Luckily no one was hurt and other than almost giving me a heart attack at the loud sound of glass breaking, I kept my cool. She was young and beautiful and a ball of nerves.

Once the food service was done, I let her go and found my way to the bar to sit next to my sister. "How's it going, Killer? You find any eye candy to take home?"

"Viv!" She hugged me, her eyes were squinting as she spoke. "You're right, that Liam guy is a hoot!" She leaned in a little closer. "And he's hot. I can't believe you aren't into him."

I glanced across the bar, watching as he ran some glasses through the sinks. He stopped the motor and turned around to place a bottle of Petron back on the high shelf. My eyes wandered to his butt just as he turned around and his eyes met mine. Nice.

Olivia also caught my stare and squealed in delight, a little too loudly. Thank you, Gray Goose. She had switched from beer to Vodka Cranberry, and I was pretty sure I would be carrying her out of the bar tonight.

"You like what you see?" She smiled at me and looked at his butt as he turned away again, pretending to squeeze his cheeks.

I swatted her hands down. "Okay, Liv, it's time to switch to water or I'll end up with a sexual harassment lawsuit."

"You don't mind, right Liam?" she said, loudly.

I felt my face heat up. I was glad she was having fun, but this was becoming too much. She was normally so reserved. I loved seeing her laugh and smile, her demeanor playful, but embarrassing me was going too far.

Liam turned around and smiled at her. "What don't I mind?"

"Vivian here staring at your sexy butt." She laughed and put her forehead on the bar.

"Water, please," I said.

He poured a glass and set it in front of her. He leaned in toward me, his elbows on the bar. "You like what you see, boss?"

My face heated up again. "I...uh..."

He laughed. "It's not often I get you tongue tied. I must be making progress."

I grabbed the rag off the bar and hit him in the shoulder with it. "Jerk."

"Hey, hey, watch the pretty face," he said, grabbing the

towel from my grasp. He brought it up to his nose and smelled it. "I'd hit you back, but this thing smells like vomit. I think you need a martini, boss."

I surprised myself when I said, "I think you're right. Make it an Apple Martini."

"You got it."

Why did I love the way boss came out of his mouth? It was like a secret nickname that made my heart pound. I was delusional and I hadn't even started drinking yet.

# CHAPTER 4

## *Liam*

VIVIAN SAT at the bar drinking with her sister. There was a lightness about her. Her loose curls were pushed behind her shoulders until she leaned forward to grab her martini and her hair fell forward. I'd never seen her smile and laugh as much as she did tonight with her sister. The music was loud, but I could hear her bubbling laugh over the bass. On her third martini, she finally stopped looking around to check out whether she was needed or not. She never took a night off, and I don't think I've ever seen her sit at the bar unless she was doing paperwork.

I picked up a rag and scrubbed the bar, making my way toward them.

"Stop looking at your phone, Olivia. Miss Hanson is more than capable of taking care of a baby. You need to relax and have a night to yourself. I'm telling you, it'll make you a better mom."

Vivian's eyes connected with mine in a silent attempt to support her. "Isn't that right, Liam?"

"What's that?"

Her eyes glowed like polished emeralds, which made my heart stumble, then race.

"Don't you think Olivia needs to have a night out since she spends every day at home taking care of her baby and hardly gets any sleep?"

I picked up their glasses and turned the motor on as I washed them through the underbar 3-compartment sink, to avoid getting lost in her beautiful eyes again. I finished and switched off the loud motor. "I think Melody's dad needs to take a turn, and you need to enjoy yourself. Your sister is right."

Vivian and Olivia exchanged glances, and they both burst out laughing.

"My daughter's father lives across the ocean. We divorced when I was pregnant, and he decided he wanted nothing to do with our baby. He just left. Vanished, to never be heard from again."

I was stunned. What man wouldn't step up and want to be a part of their child's life? I cleared my throat. "I'm sorry to hear that, but it sounds like you and your daughter dodged a bullet if he would run away from his own child. You're brave. I don't know how you do it but it's admirable."

"I have no choice," she said, looking away.

"You had a choice as much as he did except you're a better person."

Vivian nodded her head and turned toward her sister. "He's right, you know. You're so brave to do this all on your own. Now, I think you need to get out on that dance floor and dance with one of those sexy lumberjacks.

Olivia turned around to look at the dance floor. "Lumberjacks? Where do you see lumberjacks?"

"Those guys with the flannels out there," Vivian said pointing. "They look like they're from the Iron Range."

I spotted the guys she was talking about. "They do look like lumberjacks, but we call them loggers. I'm pretty sure that one guy has some pine needles on his collar.

Vivian burst out laughing and spit her martini all over my

shirt. She held her mouth. "I'm so sorry, Liam, but you're right, those are pine needles."

"My second shower of the day," I said dabbing the bar rag on my shirt.

Olivia shrugged. "I'm not interested."

"Sorry," Vivian said to me, then turned to face her sister. "Why not? They're hot!"

Olivia made a face.

Vivian gave her a look. "You aren't still thinking about that Troy guy, are you?"

Even with the dim lighting I could see Olivia's face turn red.

"You are."

"Who is Troy?" I was leaning on the bar now so as not to strain so much to hear them. I smelled Vivian's cherry shampoo.

"He's this hot widower guy from Side Lake where Olivia spent last summer."

I nodded but my blood was boiling with jealousy. What was wrong with me? Why did it bother me so much that Vivian just called a guy hot?

Olivia frowned. "He's kind and smart and sweet. You hardly spoke to him. You don't know anything."

"But his wife died. You'd always be second best. Have you guys even spoken since you left?"

Olivia gulped down the rest of her drink and avoided eye contact.

"I didn't think so. Another, please," Vivian said to me, pointing to her empty martini glass.

You could cut the tension with a knife. I had to do something. "Who wants a Chuck Norris?"

"A Chuck Norris?" Olivia said with a look of confusion.

"It's sweet, spicy, and high-energy," Vivian said. "You'll love it. I promise."

"Okay, but you're having one with me."

Vivian looked around the crowded bar. "I'm not sure."

"Go ahead, I'll drive you home. I've got this," I said. "And I can handle this crowd on my own."

She hesitated when I set the shot in front of her.

I leaned in close. I could smell the Green Apple Smirnoff on her breath, and I inhaled it. Just two more inches and I would be close enough to kiss her. But I wouldn't. I'm a gentleman, and kissing the boss would be unprofessional. I was just glad she could not see me from the waist down.

A group of women walked up to the end of the bar.

"Excuse me, hot bartender guy," the brunette said. She giggled and leaned over the bar to show her cleavage. Obviously, she was putting on a show for her friends.

I walked over with a grin. "Why hello ladies. What can I get for you."

The brunette blushed and covered her giggle. "Two vodka crans and two Jag Bombs, please." She leaned closer and grabbed the collar of my polo shirt. "Unless I can buy you a shot, too."

I glanced over at Vivian, and she nodded, a silent plea to take the shot.

I groaned and made three Jag Bombs in line, the Red Bull overflowing each glass. I grabbed my half full beer off the back counter. We clinked our glasses together. She stopped me before I raised it up to my mouth, her hand holding onto my wrist just to touch me, and smiled at me seductively. Vivian was staring at me, along with her sister.

"Hang on handsome, let me make a toast first."

I stilled.

"To the sexy bartender. May he get off early and buy me the next round."

I nodded and took the shot in my mouth then discreetly spit it into my beer bottle Vivian had shown me to do. I was getting to be a pro at it.

Vivian winked at me, seeing what I had done.

The girls slammed their shot glasses on the bar.

With watery eyes, the brunette gave me a sideways glance. "You have something right here," she said, pointing to the top of my head.

I ruffled up my hair, which was hard to do with the gel I had in it.

"No, come here," she said, making her way to the end of the bar. "Let me get it."

A trick? I worried she would try to kiss me, and I hesitated. But I was six foot three and she was maybe five foot five. I could get away if she tried anything. She was beautiful and a catch, but I was not interested. I was not the 'sleep with a girl and never call her again' type of guy.

I met her at the end of the bar, and she reached into my hair and pulled out a white fuzz ball. Was it really there or did she plant it?

"Thank you," I said, hoping she would leave me alone and let me do my job.

She grabbed onto my arm but just for a second as I turned away. I felt a sting when she squeezed my butt a little too hard. I kept walking, not paying her any attention. I would not give her another reason to call me back.

Their laughter and cheers rang in my ears as I made my way over to Vivian and Olivia. They were both pursing their lips to silence their laughter.

"How was that for you?" Vivian said with a grin.

"Don't even start. Don't forget who's driving you both home." I pointed my finger at them and let out a breath to hide my embarrassment. Note to self, never let a customer get that close again.

# CHAPTER 5

## *Vivian*

BEHIND MY LAUGH I struggled to breathe. I wanted to run over and save him. I saw the beautiful brunette's hand coming at his butt but I had no time to warn him before she pinched it. I struggled to look directly at him. I felt protective of him. I did not want him to get hurt or assaulted in my bar.

His cheeks flushed and I flashed him a real smile. It took everything in me not to run over there and kick that woman out of my bar, but I knew he could handle it. I would probably just escalate the situation since I was currently under the influence.

"My sisters saved us a seat at the bar," a voice said behind me. Tim and Lizzy joined us. Tim wrapped his arm around Olivia and my shoulders.

"You guys came."

"Couldn't pass up a chance to see you in action, Vivian."

"Have a seat. Oh, meet Liam. Liam, my brother Tim and his beautiful fiancé Lizzy." I was still wrapping my mind around my brother being engaged, let alone having a child, two children actually. I never thought he'd settle down. He enjoyed the bachelor life. Ever since we were kids, women gravitated toward him wherever he went.

"Hi, Liam. Nice to meet you. How's having my sister for a boss been? She's ruthless, right?"

I elbowed Tim in the ribs, and he groaned in fake pain.

Liam flashed me a smile that made my heart skip a beat.

"Eh, she's not so bad, but then again, I've never been elbowed in the ribs by her. You guys must share a special bond. Can I get you something to take the pain away?"

Tim nodded. "Whiskey should do it. Whatever bar pour you have."

"Your sister here owns the place and just assaulted you. I think top shelf is appropriate. Don't you think so, Vivian?"

I rolled my eyes playfully. "Fine, but you're all witnesses that I did something nice for my brother. Got it?"

Liam smirked.

"And you," I said pointing in Liam's face. "Better pour me one, too."

"Whiskey? You sure?"

I pointed at my own face. "Do I look like I'm joking?"

He poured the whiskey without another word, and Tim and I clinked glasses.

"A toast to my sister and all of her success. This place is truly amazing, and I'm so damn proud of you."

I nodded, fighting the tears in my eyes. "Okay, the sappiness is over, let's dance."

Lizzy, Olivia, and I made our way to the dance floor. The band canceled but this DJ was bringing out more people on the dance floor than our band usually did. The song choices were a hit.

Lizzy danced in the way a sober person dances when they are surrounded by a bunch of drunk people, and Olivia and I head banged to *Bohemian Rhapsody*, moon walked to *Beat It and* brought out our pointer fingers to *Dancing Queen*. When *Moulin Rouge* ended we finally called it quits. Tim and Liam had disappeared, and Alyssa appeared behind the bar.

"I wonder where those two went," I said, pointing to the empty seats.

Alyssa came over. "Liam is showing Tim your office and giving him a tour of the place."

I sobered up rather quickly and ran to my office. I had everything out on my desk. I did not expect anyone but me to go back there tonight. I busted through the door. My brother was holding the papers in his hands.

Liam's jaw dropped when I barged in. He looked so guilty. "I'm sorry, Viv. I didn't mean to, I just wanted to show your brother around."

He knew. They both knew. This was so bad.

"What is this, Viv? Why didn't you tell me?" Tim's eyes were full of concern. He was confused even though he obviously knew exactly what the papers meant. "I would have helped you."

"Give me those." I grabbed the papers out of his hand and shoved them in my desk drawer. "Why are you snooping through my stuff? This is none of your business."

Liam made his way to my office door. "I'll give you guys some privacy."

I turned to Tim, but words failed me.

He put his hand on my shoulder, and I shrugged it off.

"I know it's none of my business but how much do you owe?"

I tried to blink away the tears in my eyes. I took a deep breath, trying so hard not to cry. "The owner is selling the building so unless I buy this whole building, I'll be thrown out of here soon."

He turned me toward him. "What are you going to do?"

The tears were now running down my face. "I don't know, Tim. I've been trying to figure it out. Unless I come up with a couple hundred grand, I'll have to close this place down. I can't afford a loan. I don't have the collateral or the credit, and I don't want that debt."

His eyes widened. "No, you can't. You love this place. You've put your heart and soul into it. I don't have that much money lying around either but there has to be something we can do. How about a fundraiser or an investor or—"

I waved him off, dabbing under my eyes to wipe away black streaks running down my face. Otherwise, I would face questions when we returned to the restaurant. I was doing so well keeping it together. Now was not the time to break down.

"It's over, Tim. I've tried everything. I've known for over six months he was thinking about selling. I received the letter today that I have thirty days but they said it may be a little longer. I always hoped something would change and it wouldn't happen, but it's happening."

He started biting his nails. "There has to be something I can do to help. Anything at all to give you just a little more time."

I shook my head. "There's nothing you can do."

"What about Mom and Dad? They have the money. They would help."

"I'm a big girl. I don't need my mom and dad solving my problems and coming in to save the day. They have health issues. It's only a matter of time before they're no longer able to live in that big house by themselves. It's going to cost them a fortune for assisted living and medical care. This is my problem. And it's my restaurant, not theirs. It's my responsibility."

He put his hand on my back. "Don't give up. Let me help."

I wiped my tears and blew my nose in a tissue I grabbed from my desk.

I put my hand on his shoulder. "Tim, I love you. You're my big brother, and I appreciate that you are still trying to save me but it's over. I'm more worried about how I'm going to tell my employees. I feel terrible Liam had to find out this way.

"That's the thing about you, Vivian. You're always so worried about other people. How are you feeling about this? This was your dream. You've wanted to own your own restaurant since we were kids and you've done it. You have a successful business. How about moving it to another location? There has to be a way."

I stared at him, my expression angry. "Tim, drop it, please. Let's go back out there and have some fun and leave the trouble in the office. I don't want to talk about this right now. I want to have a fun night with my sister and my brother and my soon to be sister-in-law."

He put his head down in surrender and held the bridge of his nose between his thumb and pointer finger. One eye peeked at me. "Fine, but we'll have this conversation another day."

"Fine," I said, leading the way to my office door. I held it open for him and followed him out.

"Another round of shots, please." I told Alyssa when we reached the bar.

"No more for me," Olivia said, waving off the bartender.

"Me neither, I'm good," Tim said.

"Then give me theirs," I said. "Three shots of Fireball."

A look of concern crossed Alyssa's face, but she said, "Coming right up."

My whole demeanor changed, and where the hell was Liam? He had disappeared.

I downed all three shots one after the other, hoping to forget about my problems for the night. Tim's eyes reflected his concern. I hated the sad look on his face. He needed to let it go. This was not his battle to fight.

"Who wants to dance?" I grabbed Olivia's hand, and she laughed but followed me without a fight.

Lizzy yelled out," I love this song!" And she was right behind Olivia.

I'm not sure how long we danced, but I danced and drank until the altercation in my office was no longer on my mind. We sang into our fists and let loose until the music stopped, and the lights dimmed, announcing the bar was closing.

"How about an after bar at my house," I said locking arms with Lizzy and Olivia.

"I'd love to but I'm exhausted. I'm up way past my bedtime and these twins take all my energy," Lizzy said as she patted her slim belly.

"And I need to get some sleep, too. Melody doesn't care how late I stay up. She'll be up in just a few hours." Olivia turned to Lizzy. "Can I catch a ride with you and Tim? You guys are staying at Mom and Dad's, right?"

She nodded. "Absolutely."

We walked up to the bar where Tim, Liam, and Alyssa were all chatting.

Tim hugged me. "How are you getting home, Viv? Need a ride?"

"I'm driving her," Liam said. "Alyssa is closing up the bar tonight."

"Are you sure, Alyssa?" I tried to focus on her but everything was blurry, and I was feeling a bit queasy from the shots. I'm pretty sure I had three too many.

"Thank you so much for inviting us. I had a blast," Lizzy said, her hand on her belly again. She was hardly showing but she obviously loved being pregnant.

"My pleasure. Don't be a stranger," I said and hugged her.

Tim forced a smile my way and whispered in my ear, "Call me."

I nodded and fought not to start crying again. I tried not to think about it. This bar was my life, and I was losing it.

Liam split the tips before grabbing my jacket and putting it on me. I turned toward him as he zipped me up. I was too drunk and the room was spinning. I wanted to fight him, tell him I could do it myself, but I could hardly stay upright without leaning on something.

"You okay?"

I nodded, but I was not okay. I would never be okay. The alcohol would soon be out of my system, but the problems would never go away.

I tripped on the rug before we reached the back door. I waited for Liam to say something but instead he picked me up and carried me like a bride all the way to his car. I was too drunk to even yell at him to put me down.

# CHAPTER 6

## *Liam*

I **SET** Vivian down before opening the passenger door and helping her in. She just sat there, not moving so I reached across to buckle her in. Her arm raised to my face as I was backing away. I turned toward her and stared into her eyes. I hated to see her so broken, her dreams falling apart in front of her eyes.

I leaned close and rested my head against hers and softly whispered, "You're so beautiful. Do you know that? Inside and out."

I wanted to say something, tell her how I felt, but she was drunk, and not thinking straight. It took everything I had to keep my mouth shut, so instead of telling her how I really felt, I just smiled. Now was not the right time.

She smiled back and touched my lip with her thumb. She was staring at my lips.

I wanted to see what those lips felt like on mine, but I had enough self-control to move away.

She dropped her hand on her thigh with a slap. "And that smile. I love that smile," she mumbled. "That face, your body. The way you—"

I cut off her words when I shut the door and took a deep

breath. She mumbled something but I tried not to listen. This woman was torture, and turning her down would take every ounce of strength I had. Her words were not real, she was just rambling and probably was unsure of who she was even talking to at this point.

I took another deep breath before opening up my door and getting in the car. Her head was on her shoulder, her eyes closed. Seconds later she began snoring.

We were several blocks from her house when she jumped in her seat and turned her head in panic. "Liam, do you have a ba—"

Before she could get another word out, she vomited on my lap. A rancid smell filled the car, and I held my breath as I held up her hair because the thought of her getting vomit in her hair was my biggest concern.

She continued hacking in my lap until nothing was left in her stomach. She wiped her mouth and put her head against the window. The smell of whiskey and rancid apples filled my nostrils. I rolled down my window just enough to get the fresh air to circulate the car. My lap was sticky and wet. When I pulled up at her house and got out of the car, my lap instantly froze from the freezing temperature outside.

Before I got to her side of the car, Vivian was already out her door and crawling on all fours through the snow. I reached down to grab her under the arms and pull her to her feet.

"No offense, Liam," she slurred. "But you smell terrible."

I shook my head and laughed at her. "Yeah, I should probably take a shower. I did get some vomit on me."

"Yeah. That's gross."

I picked her up again and carried her to her door. "Keys?"

Her eyes rolled in the back of her head. "They're in my

pocket," she said. "Looks like you'll have to find them." How could I get mad when she was acting so cute?

I set her down but held her arm. She made no attempt to pull her keys out of her pocket, so I did it for her. I held my breath, trying not to touch her thigh as I fished out the keys.

"Oh, Liam. My sweet Liam," she sang with a drunken smile.

Even drunk she was so beautiful and adorable. The paper flashed through my head. That was the reason for how much she'd been drinking lately. She was going to lose the bar unless I did something. But how was I going to save the bar without her knowing? She would never let me help her. She had no idea how much money I had, or she would be wondering why I worked at her bar. I definitely was not there for the money.

I carried her up to her bedroom and set her down on the bed then I stripped off my vomit-stained jacket and threw it into a ball on the floor.

"Do you want to try to brush your teeth?"

She nodded.

I helped her take her jacket off and she stood up and started sliding her pants off. I turned away to be a gentleman and opened up her dresser drawers to find her some comfy pants. Most of the vomit was on me, not her, just a bit on her jacket and her jeans.

The springs of the bed squeaked. She was sitting on the edge without any pants on. I grabbed the flannel pants and slid them up each leg, careful to look away. Then I put my arm around her and led her to the bathroom where I grabbed her toothbrush and put some toothpaste on it. She did a good job brushing her teeth by herself, but her eyes were rolling around and twice she almost fell over, but I tightened my grip.

I led her back to the bed and tucked her in.

"Good night, Liam. Thank you for taking care of me. You are the bestest."

"Do you mind if I jump in your shower quick?"

She mumbled something and I heard her snore again. I was pretty sure she would not care since I was covered in her vomit, so I went into her bathroom and found a towel. I kept the door open six inches to hear in case she got sick again. I did not want her to choke on her vomit.

I let the water run then got into the shower. I grabbed the bar of soap and smelled it, taking a deep breath. It smelled like cherries, just like her. She smelled so damn good. I rubbed the soap all over me and in my hair, then a loud noise startled me. I opened the shower door and peeked into the bedroom where I left her on the bed, but she was no longer in there. I finished getting the soap out of my hair and turned off the shower.

"Leave it on," she said, making her way toward me.

I grabbed the towel as fast as I could and wrapped it around her naked body, then shielded my groin with my t-shirt off the floor.

"Viv, what are you doing?"

"I smell," she slurred. "I need a shower. Why do I smell like puke?" She pulled on her towel and I turned away and started the shower for her. I had no choice. She was getting in there no matter what I said.

I looked away once she stepped into the shower. I turned my back and dug my fingers into my eyeballs to stop the overflowing thoughts racing through my brain. I switched out the shirt for a towel and tied it around my waist. I was stuck and I didn't know what to do. She finally finished her shower after what felt like forever, and when the water shut off, I closed my eyes and held the towel out for her. She wrapped it around her body, but she stumbled getting out of the shower and I had to catch her.

I felt like such a creeper, unable to wipe away the naked image of her when she walked toward me. I closed my eyes but not before getting a full view. I could never tell her what happened. She would be so embarrassed that I saw her naked. How could I have been so stupid? I should have locked the bathroom door.

She refused to get dressed before slipping under the covers, so I once again turned my head and pulled the comforter over her. I took my jeans into her laundry room and threw them in the wash. I would never fit into any of her clothes, but I was not going to put those rancid pants back on. I sat in the chair in her bedroom in just my towel until my alarm woke me up to change over my laundry. I threw them in the dryer and went back upstairs to sit in the chair again. I checked on her, she looked so peaceful in her bed. She was smiling in her sleep. I stared for a little too long before ripping my eyes away from her and grabbing the blanket off the end of her bed to cover myself up. I needed more than a towel to keep me warm.

The sound of the drier buzzing woke me from a deep sleep. It took me a minute to remember where I was until I saw her sweet face peeking out from the top of the comforter. Her face brought on a smile even though my neck had a bad kink in it from sleeping in the chair all night and my long legs were stiff. I stood up to stretch before I made my way to the drier.

When I came back upstairs, she was still out cold. To save her the embarrassment of seeing me in her room babysitting when she woke up, I put on my jacket, kissed her cheek to make sure she was still breathing and warm, and tiptoed out of the room and into my cold car.

I covered my mouth with my fist and hit the steering wheel twice before starting up the car and pulling out onto the road. I left my heart with her in that room. I was going to make this right. She would not lose her restaurant. Not over my dead body. I would find a way to save the building. I just needed to come up with a plan.

# CHAPTER 7
## *Vivian*

EVERYTHING HURT. My legs were cramped, my eyes struggled to open. With my arms above my head I did a sniff test. I smelled like cherries. Did I take a shower last night? I searched the bed, looking beneath the sheets to make sure I had not made a dumb decision. Why was I naked?

Think…

I remembered laughing at the bar with my brother and sister. My chest stiffened and I sat straight up in bed. The papers, Tim found the papers on my desk. Damn Liam for showing my brother my office. I flopped down on the bed and covered my eyes with my comforter and let out a loud grunt of frustration that turned into a frustrated scream.

"Damn it!" I punched the mattress beside me and shielded my eyes from the bright sun. My head hurt so much. How the hell did I get home?

A gorgeous face popped into my head.

Liam.

Hopefully, I did not say anything too terrible or embarrassing. If I did, I'd be hearing about it today. And when did I get naked? Long after he was gone, I hoped.

My phone vibrated on the bedside table. I picked it up to see Olivia's name appear on the screen.

"Okay, how drunk was I last night?"

She laughed. "Good morning to you, Sis. How are you feeling this morning?"

I sighed. "Like I was hit by a truck."

"Sounds about right. I'm feeling the same way. Why didn't I drink more water?"

"How's that baby?"

"She's good. I just got her to sleep, and I couldn't wait to call and hear all about your drive home with that hot bar manager of yours. Why were you holding out on me? How come you never mentioned him??"

"Oh, Liam? It's not like that." I stood up and my legs wobbled a bit beneath me. "He's just Liam."

"Just Liam? You have to be kidding me. Why haven't you made a move on him?"

I tapped the speaker phone and slid on my pants. When exactly did I take them off? Nor could I recall even getting into bed last night. "He's not my type."

"He's everyone's type."

I glanced in the mirror to find my mascara smeared under my bloodshot eyes. "He's my employee, Liv. And he's like a brother to me." Okay, maybe not like a brother. I definitely did not have thoughts like that about Tim. Gross.

"He sure doesn't look like he thinks of you as a sister. Don't let him get away, Viv. He was so sweet to take you home last night."

The memory of him carrying me into my house like a child popped into my head. Oh no. "He's too normal for me anyway. You know I always tend to be attracted to the assholes. It's inevitable, really."

She snorted.

"I'm glad you think my men issues are funny."

"You should give him a chance."

"Enough about Liam. If you like him then you date him."

The line went silent. Olivia was too busy crushing on Troy to make a move on Liam.

"Well, anyway, I'm going to take a nap, and I'll be home this afternoon. I haven't drank like that in quite some time. Tim and Lizzy were heading back to Side Lake today, but I haven't heard if they've left or not. Have you heard from them?"

"Nope." And I hoped Tim would not call me. I would never hear the end of my restaurant going down. I did not want to deal with it right now.

"Okay, well I guess I'll see you tonight. Are you working?"

"I'll probably go in for a little bit before I play volleyball."

"Well, you should really think about the possibility of Liam, I'm just saying. Maybe try dating someone who is nice and not a complete jerk. Just a thought."

If only I was attracted to the good ones. Yes, he was easy on the eyes, but our relationship was not like that. Nor did Liam see me that way. He joked around and we flirted a little back and forth, but nothing more than that. We'd never cross that line. But the thought of having a conversation about the restaurant would give me a heart attack. He loved the place almost as much as I did.

"I'll think about it," I said in a dismissing tone. "Bye, Sis. Now get some sleep before your daughter wakes up."

"You don't have to tell me twice."


I walked into my bar with a pounding headache and wearing big sunglasses. Liam's face lit up when he saw me come in.

"Princess, did you have a tough night?"

I pushed my sunglasses up on my head and rolled my eyes. "Yes, I had a bartender who over served me last night. I think he should be fired."

He poured me a Bloody Mary and put an extra pickle on the toothpick. "Poor baby. What you happened to forget is that he was such a gentleman he not only drove your drunk butt home but tucked you into bed. How many bartenders would do that without taking advantage of you?"

My mouth dropped. "Oh, shit. I was hoping that was a dream and I took an Uber or something."

He winked at me. "I didn't mind one bit, boss.."

Why was it when he called me boss it made me instantly blush. The way he said it. The way he smiled so confidently. The way his voice sounded, and his attention was on me and only me. Did he see me naked? No. He'd say something, right? Would I even be upset? The thought of his arms around me and his lips against mine sent a chill down my spine. But he was not my type. Nothing would happen. He was my employee. Not only my employee but the best damn employee I ever had, even if only for a few more weeks until the bar closed. The thought made my heart sink.

"We need to have a talk," I whispered. "About what you saw last night."

He looked down. His broad, confident stance now strained, and his shoulders hunched.

"I don't know what you're talking about," he said to make light of the conversation. He flashed me that flirty smile, a sparkle back in his eyes.

I frowned and motioned for him to follow me as I made my way back to my office. His footsteps sounded heavy behind me. I let him in and shut the door behind him.

He put his hand out to stop me. "You don't need to explain. This is really none of my business. I never should have let your brother into your office without asking you first. I'm sorry—"

"No. This is not on you. You did nothing wrong. You've been my best employee, and I know you're also running your own business on the side." I stopped to catch my breath.

A noise startled me from behind and Alyssa came rushing in. "Vivian, someone's on the phone for you."

I waved her off. "Take a message."

Her face filled with concern. "He said it's important and it's regarding the restaurant."

"Shit. I'll be right there."

Alyssa nodded and shut the door.

"We'll resume this conversation later."

He nodded. "I'll wait."

"No, go back to work. We can talk later. I have to get this."

He ran his fingers through his hair nervously. "Okay."

How sweet that he cared.

I raced into the bar and picked up the phone. "Hello, this is Vivian."

"Vivian, it's Justin at the bank. I wanted to make sure you got my letter in the mail."

"I did."

"I'm really sorry to hear about your business. I wish I had some better news for you."

I pushed my back against the wall, my body was so weak I struggled to stand without collapsing. "Yeah, me too." I wanted to scream at him, tell him this was not fair, and I needed more time, but this mess was not his fault. He was just doing his job."

When I hung up the phone, Liam was right there. He looked at me with concern in his eyes, and he pulled me in for a hug. He smelled so good, like cedar and a hint of cherries. Cherries? I breathed him in and squeezed him tighter.

He pulled away and looked into my eyes. "Is there anything I can do to help? Name it."

His beautiful eyes held mystery, but I was too broken to question him. I whispered, "Can we get out of here? I need some air and I need to be anywhere but here right now." I squeezed my arms around his back, my heart pounding in my chest.

"How about I take you to Canal Park and get some sushi? Take your mind off all this."

I nodded. "I could use a distraction right now. Take me anywhere but here."

"As you wish."

# CHAPTER 8

## *Liam*

WE WALKED into Cloud 9 and got seated in a booth. I struggled to think because defeat was written all over Vivian's face, and my heart ached for her.

"What would you like to drink?" I asked, peeking at her over the menu.

"Red wine sounds good. I'm thinking a cabernet."

"I'll have one, too," I said.

She shut her menu. "I'm not sure why I even open a menu when I always have the same thing."

"What's that?"

"Spicy machi combo. I love my sushi rolls." She leaned in and whispered, "And if I'm really feeling daring, I get the shrimp hibachi."

I laughed. "I won't tell anyone. I always get the same thing, too."

She eyed me suspiciously. "And what's that."

I flashed her my sexiest smile. "Well, usually I start with a mango boba tea, then I order a Dragon Roll and a Rainbow Roll." I leaned in closer to imitate her. "And sometimes when I'm feeling daring, I also get Shrimp Hibachi."

She smiled and looked around. "I just love this place."

"You're glowing."

"What?"

"You're glowing."

She opened her mouth to speak but the waiter interrupted us and took our order. Once he left, I took her hand in mine and squeezed it. I expected her to pull away, but she surprised me and squeezed me back.

"I've put my heart and soul into my restaurant. The thought of losing it just breaks me." She put her head down and it took everything for me not to get up and put my arms around her again. I held my breath. "Viv, I—"

"Here you go," the waiter said as he handed us our drinks. "I brought you some waters, too."

I nodded. "Thank you."

He walked away and I struggled to find my words to continue.

"What were you saying?"

I shook my head. "I think we should have a fundraiser. See if we can raise enough money for a downpayment on a loan or even raise enough money to open up your restaurant at another location. What do you think?"

She shook her head. "I don't know if a fundraiser will be enough, but Liam, I don't tell you often enough how much I appreciate you and all you do. Zenith Bar and Grill wouldn't be what it was if it wasn't for your help. I know you have your own business, and I want you to know I notice. I notice you working late hours during tax season and how exhausted your eyes look when you come to the bar right after work. I see you, Liam, and I'm grateful for all you've done and continue to do for my restaurant."

"Zenith is my home, and I love working with you and the rest of our crew. It may seem weird, but the bar is my outlet. It's how I destress after a long day of punching numbers. I love your restaurant, and I'm not ready to give up on it yet."

She laughed and shook her head at me.

"What?" I smiled back. "I think we should try."

"How did I get so lucky? You aren't just an employee to me, you're a friend. A great friend. I don't know what I'd do without you." She laughed and shook her head again. "I mean we only have thirty days. Are you sure you want to do this?"

Did I have the time to put into a fundraiser so last minute like this? No. Tax season left me no time for anything, but I could never let her down. She needed me and I needed her. Since she came into my life, I've never been happier. Her smile brought me up on the darkest of days. She was my person, and I would do what I had to do to save the restaurant. "I'm sure."

"Okay, then I guess we're doing this. I'm not excited about breaking the news to everyone but I know I need to do it right away so we can focus on saving my restaurant."

I was unable to tell this woman no. Did she know that? Whatever her dreams, I would help her make them come true.

I placed my hand on her lower back as I followed her out the door after dinner. "Have anywhere you need to be?"

She looked at her watch. "Not for a couple hours. Why?"

"Let's take a walk down the lakewalk and see the shops at Fitger's. What do you say?" Fitger's was an old brewery built over a hundred years ago. I loved strolling through it.

She batted her eyelashes, deep in thought, and I found myself staring at her lips. I turned away before it got awkward.

"That sounds nice. I don't remember the last time I slowed down enough to take a walk on the Duluth Lakewalk and enjoyed the scenery. It really is so beautiful by the lake."

The wind off Lake Superior blew her curly hair in front of her face as we made our way through the parking lot at Caribou Coffee and past the hotel to the lakewalk. Once on the trail, we stopped for a good look at the lighthouse in the distance.

Vivian wrapped her arms around her midsection, her shoulders stiffened.

I took off my jacket and placed it over her shoulders. She smiled. "Thank you."

We both took a seat on the bench that faced Lake Superior, and I put my arm around her. In return, she rested her head on my shoulder and snuggled into the nook of my neck.

I had a thick sweatshirt on underneath my Carheart jacket, so I was still warm enough after I gave it to her.

Despite being spring, the air was still a bit chilly and scattered patches of snow lay on the ground. Soon it would be muddy, and walking would become an obstacle course. Luckily the blacktop on the bike trail portion of the trail was newly paved, and the walking trail that ran parallel to Lake Superior was a wooden path for walkers. The two paths ran parallel to each other and the lake. The boulders were the only thing in between the sidewalk and the lake. We both stared at the waves that splashed into the shore in front of us.

We sat for a few minutes before the wind got so cold we decided to walk again. I swung my arms to stay warm, and we picked up our pace. The word Fitger's stuck out on the building in the distance. It looked so close yet so far away, just like my relationship with Vivian. I reached out to grab her icy cold hand.

Our eyes met and she smiled. "When I found out I had to shut down the restaurant, I was broken. I couldn't sleep and I was drank more than I should have to try to numb the pain. I was hurt, Liam. I had a hard time catching my breath. Now you've made me feel hope."

We stopped on the bridge, the wind no longer blowing in our face, and leaned over the railing to gaze into the water. I put her hands to my mouth and blew warm air on her frozen fingers. "We've got this. It will be a lot of work, but I know we can do it."

She nodded. "Thank you for helping me when I was ready to give up. We may not be able to save the restaurant, but at least we'll know we did everything we could." She turned away and wiped her face with the back of her hand.

I wanted to take all of her pain away. It was so hard to see her this way. I pulled her chin up. "I'm right here by your side and we're going to fight like crazy to keep it."

She headed down the path again, and I followed. Two runners passed by at a steady pace. I ached to get back into running again. With how busy I was during tax season, I had to give a lot up. I considered cutting back my hours at the restaurant but giving up time with Vivian was not an option for me. She was the highlight of my day, everyday.

"I'm just exhausted and scared. Everyone is going to be so upset. This is their livelihood."

"That's true but maybe they'll surprise you."

"Maybe."

"Don't worry about it tonight. We'll come up with a plan to tell the staff, then it's up to them whether they want to stick around and help save the restaurant or if they want to leave."

We climbed the concrete staircase and crossed the bridge until we reached the Fitger's building. I opened the door for her as she slipped past me into the warmth.

Vivian stared at the walls and the hallway with such curiosity. She reached out and touched the brick wall. "Do you ever feel like we let life pass us by without taking in the beauty that is all around us?" She slipped off her shoes and smiled at me. Who knew a smile could warm my entire body?

"I never thought about it that way." I was curious about why she took off her shoes.

She threw her arms in the air and spun in a circle, smiling as if she was having the best day of her life. I smiled at her curiously. The stares of the passersby did not catch her attention. I watched in awe.

"I love the vaulted ceilings in here, the historical beauty around every corner. It's just such a cornerstone of Duluth and our community. From prohibition and post-war brewing, this building has so much to say. If only the walls could talk. What do you think they would tell us?"

I touched the brick alongside her. Our fingers lightly touched but neither of us moved our hands away. Her words made me see this building in a whole new way.

"Did you know when prohibition began in 1920, most breweries closed over the next thirteen years, but Fitger's survived those odds. They diversified their brewery and introduced pop and candy bars. Duluth savored their candy bars. My grandmother told me Fitger's Skookum was the best candy bar of them all. A bully good bar they called it. Wasn't that a creative name? Locals would take Lovit Pops, which were one of their most popular drinks, to Park Point where they enjoyed them on hot summer days."

"I didn't realize that." I ran my hand through my hair and took in the scenery with new eyes.

"My grandmother told me they closed in the 1970's but Fitger's beer was still sold at Shell's Brewing Company in New Ulm, Minnesota into the 80's."

"Yeah, I know this building was almost demolished when I-35 was extended but the community and the leaders around here fought to make sure the historic buildings weren't destroyed and instead, preserved," I said.

"This didn't become a retail space with restaurants, shops, a theater, and a museum until the 80's. There have been a lot of renovations and new owners since this building was first built. So many upgrades until it finally transformed into the thriving historical place it is today. We take for granted what is right here in front of us."

She was so beautiful when she was passionate about

something. This was a deeper side of her than I'd ever seen. Who knew she could get me to care so much for this old building I had been in a million times? Just when I thought I could not fall any harder for her, she proved me wrong.

"Why did you take your shoes off? Aren't you cold?"

"It's the way I ground myself. Feel the earth beneath my feet. It calms me. Usually, I do it in the grass but that isn't an option this time of year."

She was so cute. It made no sense to me, but I did not care. Everything about this woman was mysterious to me. She was unlike any woman I'd ever known. She was just my Vivian.

# CHAPTER 9

## *Vivian*

BOOKSTORE AT FITGER'S was eye catching from the moment I walked in the door. Books were scattered throughout the store, and every book had an adventure or a trip just waiting to be dived into. The worker's face lit up as she peeked at me over the big box of books she was holding in her arms. "Can I help you find anything?"

Her warm welcome as I walked into the enchanting bookstore made me smile. I pointed to the side along the counter. "I think I see exactly where I need to be."

Liam walked behind me. The aisles around the books were small, and I had to move to the side to let a woman pass me, but the setting was perfect and quaint. I ran my hands over the spines of books in the romance section. Once my favorite genres, though I had not read a romance book in years. I no longer believed in a perfect man and these books felt like lies, false hope. I'd grown out of Disney stories years ago.

Liam leaned over my shoulder and whispered, "You like romance books?" His voice almost sounded hopeful.

"Used to."

"Used to as in you don't have a chance to read anymore

with your busy schedule? Or used to as in you no longer like them at all?"

"I just outgrew them. They're fairytales."

He turned me toward him. "Romance books aren't fairytales. They're love stories. Don't tell me you've given up believing in love."

I no longer felt like buying a book. "Let's go." I guided him through the narrow walkway and out the door of the bookstore.

"I think love is actually people settling. It doesn't last. We all fall out of love eventually."

His eyebrows rose and his face showed only disappointment. "Wait, aren't your parents still together?"

"Yeah. So?"

"Well, you grew up watching them. Aren't they still in love?"

I laughed. "They're still together, but I wouldn't say they're in love. Marriage is more of a partnership with them. A business transaction of sorts."

His eyes widened as if he couldn't believe the words coming out of my mouth. Someone needed to help this poor, naïve guy.

"Look, my parents support each other, but they settled just like the rest of Americans who stay in a marriage for over thirty years. My dad owned his own business and made good money, and my mom was good at finances. She held the house together while he worked. He was never home much when I was growing up. My mom was kind of the mom and the dad for us. She took us to our sports and drove us around in the minivan while my dad took us fishing sometimes on the weekends and did the best he could. Don't get me wrong, I had a good childhood. There were six of us and my parents made sure we never went without. They were good parents."

"But? I definitely hear a but coming."

I followed him up the stairs to the next floor. "But I think they settled. I never saw my parents kiss, and they never really fought either. They raised us all together and did a good job and now they help take care of each other. My mom's health isn't good, she has diabetes, and my dad has his own issues. There's just…no passion between them."

"Just because they don't flaunt it doesn't mean there's no passion."

He was such a hopeful romantic. "Have you had your heart broken, Liam?"

"A few times."

"And you still believe in love?"

"Absolutely."

We walked by a cafe and stopped to get a coffee before finally making our way to the parking lot and back to the lakewalk.

"Are your parents madly in love? Because I hate to break it to you, but they're probably just putting on a show."

He stopped walking and turned to look at the lake. "My parents died in a car accident when I was sixteen years old."

"I'm so sorry, I didn't know, Liam. I'm such a jerk." My jaw dropped in shock. His parents died when he was a teenager? How devastating.

He shook his head and put his arm around me as he pulled me in.

"No, not at all. You didn't know. I don't really talk about it. But they were madly in love. What they had I have chased my whole life, and I know it's out there for me. I'm not going to settle or give into anything less than what they had."

"That's beautiful. I'm so sorry about your parents. That must have been so hard for you." I'd put my foot in my mouth which seemed to be a normal occurrence lately around him.

He dropped his arm, and I wrapped my arm around his and snuggled close to warm up.

"Dealing with my grief was not easy, but my aunt and

uncle took me in without a second thought. My parents had it in their will that my sister and I would go to them if anything were to happen, and they honored that. I owe them everything. They also never settled and have a great marriage. I guess I was always surrounded by people in love."

"They sound like amazing people."

"But I haven't changed your mind on believing in love, have I?"

I felt my face go hot even though I was chilled to the bone from the cold wind coming off the lake. "They sound like selfless people for what they did for you, but I still don't believe in love. I'm sorry, I can't lie to you."

I looked over to see him smiling at me. "Let me take you for dinner at their house. I want you to meet them and then you can be the judge whether or not true love exists.

"Liam, are you tricking me into going on a date with you?"

"I don't know. Did it work?"

"Absolutely. Let's make a bet."

"What kind of bet?"

What was I doing? Would he ever forgive me when I met them and still did not believe they were in love? I'd just hurt him. I could not do that to him. "Never mind," I said. "It's not a good idea."

"What? Why?"

"Because these are your people and who am I to judge in just an hour or so of meeting them? It seems wrong."

He stopped walking and took both of my hands in his, rubbing them to warm them up.

"I'm not worried about it. If you have a meal with us and don't think they're in love then I'll drop this and never bother you again about your disbelief in true love, but if I'm right then you have to promise to stop saying you don't believe in love."

He was never going to win but if he was insistent I would

not turn down the competition. A big part of me, and I hated to admit it, wanted to meet the amazing humans who helped raise him.

"Deal," I said, shaking his hand. "Now, let's walk faster, I'm so cold and I need to get to volleyball."

"Do you ever have a night to yourself?"

"Nope. I like to stay busy. It keeps the mind from going insane."

# CHAPTER 10

## *Liam*

I MADE my way back to my downtown office and got right to work. Taxes were piling up, and I needed to get back on track. I never expected a part time job to become my priority, but I wanted to be with Vivian. Her sadness made my heart ache, and I was on a mission to fix her. That was a terrible way to think about it. Maybe help her was a better way to put it. She needed optimism, not fixing.

"Liam, is that you? Where have you been? You're going to be filing extensions like crazy if you don't start pulling your weight."

"Nice to see you too, Rog," I said, pulling his head under my arm and rustling up his hair. Roger was my cousin but also more like a brother to me. His parents raised me, after all. He went from being their only child to sharing all the attention with me and my sister. We butted heads a lot when we were younger, but now we were definitely brothers.

"What's going on? Don't tell me you were working at the bar all day again. You do know you make enough money as an accountant not to take on another job, right?"

"You know I love it. It's not about the money."

"I think there's something you aren't telling me. Actually, Mom and Dad called me today and invited me to dinner tomorrow night. They said you're bringing a date? This woman doesn't happen to be a customer at the bar, does she? Is this the real reason you've been working there so much?"

"Vivian is not a customer. She's just a friend."

He squinted at me, a look of disbelief on his face. "Just a friend, huh? Then why are you blushing."

"I'm not blushing." Was I?

His smile widened like the joker. "You are now."

I punched him lightly in the shoulder, and he grimaced. "I wasn't going to go since it's tax season and I'm spread thin already trying to cover both your load and mine, but now I don't think I could miss it."

I shook my head and walked away from him and into my office. I'd never hear the end of it if he found out she was my boss.

Three in the morning, I woke up drooling on my desk. I rubbed my eyes and made my way to the couch. I needed a couple hours of sleep before I hit the numbers again. A slamming office door woke me around eight.

"Are you still here? Why are you sleeping on the couch?"

Roger was showered and had two coffees from the Duluth Coffee Company in his hand.

"I needed a quick nap. Is that for me?" I said, pointing to the coffees.

"Yeah, I figured you wouldn't make it home last night. We've got pop tarts in the cupboard if you're hungry."

"Pop tarts? How old do you think I am?"

"Fine, don't have any. Ari was kind enough to share them with you but if you aren't hungry, I'll eat them."

My sister was our secretary, and she did a damn good job even though she mainly worked remote. She loved pop tarts and kept the cupboard stocked.

I jumped up and held out my arm. "Don't you dare. I'm hungry as hell and if you take even one bite I may have to fight you for it."

He raised his arms in surrender. "It's all yours, man. Now get to work. Don't forget to shower before your big date tonight. I can't wait to meet her."

Tonight would be a disaster, I just knew it.


I showed up at her door with yellow flowers because I had to bring her something, but I did not want to scare her away. Yellow roses stood for friendship, joy, and warmth. In no way did I want her to panic if I brought her something more romantic. She had finally agreed to go on a date with me. I had to move slowly and not scare her away.

Olivia opened up the door with a baby in her arms and a giant grin from ear to ear. She looked me up and down. "Well, don't you clean up nice, Mr. Bartender."

I wiped my feet on the rug and shook my head at her. "Great to see you again, Olivia. Is this the beautiful little girl you've been bragging about? I can see why."

"Liam, meet Melody. You caught her on a good day. She's clean and smells like baby because she just got out of the bath." In a higher voice she said, "Didn't you sweet girl? You smell so good. Don't you?"

My body instantly heated up. I unzipped my jacket halfway and fanned my face.

Olivia looked up at me. "Are you okay? You look like you're going to pass out. Come in, have a seat. You're suddenly flush."

I took off my shoes and sat down on a chair.

"Thank you. That was odd."

"I was a nurse for many years. A man passing out is something I know a lot about. Let me get you a glass of water."

I thought about stopping her. Her hands were full with the baby, and I was a grown man, but I was worried I'd pass out if I stood up right now.

She walked around the corner and came back with a glass of ice water.

"I'll be out in just one minute, I'm brushing my teeth quick," I heard Vivian call out as she dashed down the hallway.

"No rush, I'm early," I said.

"I think she's a little nervous. This isn't something she usually does." Olivia's voice turned to a low whisper. "The truth is she never meets her boyfriends' parents."

"We aren't dating," I said.

She smiled as if she knew a secret and she was hiding it from me.

"Oh, I know. Vivian has made that clear, but I see the way you look at each other. Mark my words, the two of you will be together one day."

My body heated up again and I took another sip of water.

"Look at you squirming over there. How are you going to get through a whole dinner with her without passing out? Like I said, I'm a nurse. Maybe I should come with you, just to make sure you don't pass out," she said in a teasing voice.

I heard a door open down the hallway and Vivian appeared. She was dressed in jeans and an oversized green sweater. The sweater was big but did little to hide her tiny frame. The truth was I couldn't wait to show her off to my parents. She was beautiful and kind and funny. Once she met my parents she would think about love differently. Anyone who met them did.

"You're stunning, Vivian."

She blushed and grabbed her jacket off the hook behind her. "Thank you. Are you ready to go?"

I stood up and followed her to the car. I ran ahead to open the door for her.

"You didn't need to do that, Liam."

"I know but I can't help it, my parents raised me to be a gentleman."

She shook her head and sat in the passenger seat. I smiled at her and closed the door. Damn I was lucky. I just needed to play it cool and not screw up tonight.

# CHAPTER 11

## *Vivian*

WE PULLED up beside a small house. I followed Liam up the sidewalk to the porch. He knocked twice and peeked his head in.

"Hello, anyone home? Mom, Dad?"

We stomped our feet before stepping into the entryway and taking off our shoes. I followed Liam into a small but uncluttered kitchen.

His mother had a cute red apron on with polka dots. "Liam, honey, you're here." She leaned around him to get a better look at me. "And this must be the famous Vivian."

I smiled and reached my hand out to shake hers but instead she pulled me into a hug. She smelled like chocolate chip cookies and the delicious smell of pasta lingered in my nose.

I hugged her back gently. She was so tiny I was afraid if I squeezed her too hard, I would break something. "I don't know about famous but it's so great to meet you Ms. Nyman. I've heard so much about you."

"Liam never brings anyone home so please, take a seat. I'd love to hear more about you and who this mystery lady is that my son actually invited over for dinner. It's truly a pleasure to have you here."

The door opened from outside and an older version of Liam walked in the door. If I didn't know this man was his uncle and not his father, I would have never guessed. He was dark and handsome, a couple inches taller than Liam but the same perfect smile and strong jawline. He held a bouquet of pink lilies and red roses. He handed the bouquet out to his wife and her face lit up.

"Oh, Michael, you shouldn't have. What are these for?" She blushed and sniffed the flowers. They kissed just a little longer than I expected. My stomach fluttered.

"I thought a little color would brighten up the table and although nothing could ever be as beautiful as you are, I knew it would brighten up your day. And make you smile."

She leaned in and whispered, " I'm so glad you did. Thank you."

Normally stuff like this would make me want to vomit, but he was so genuine. For a moment they acted like the rest of us did not exist. They only saw each other. Liam cleared his throat which snapped them out of the world they were in.

"How rude of me. Michael, this is Liam's friend Vivian. Vivian, meet my husband, Michael."

Michael took off his shoes and came over to hug me. His parents were so kind and the hugs genuine. They were easy to be around, and I felt like I'd known them my whole life. I glanced at Liam, and he flashed me a cocky smile. He thought he was winning, and I hated to admit it, but he was right.

My thoughts skidded to a halt. No. One bouquet of flowers meant nothing. I did not suddenly believe in love. Maybe Liam's father did something bad, and he was apologizing with flowers. Maybe it was more of a mutual respect, a partnership.

As soon as we sat down at the kitchen table, big blue eyes came around the corner.

"Just in time for dinner, Roger. Why don't you sit down by Vivian over here. Have you two met?"

Roger put out his hand, and I shook it.

"I'm Roger. You're even more beautiful than Liam led on. I can see why he has been falling behind on his work." He pulled my hand to his lips and kissed it.

Liam shot daggers at his brother. "Be nice, Rog," he said through clenched teeth. "Hands off."

"You know I'm just kidding." Roger turned to look at me. "He's always behind on his work during tax season. It's nothing new."

So, he was falling behind at work. Because of me? Here I was putting even more pressure on him to help me with a last-minute fundraiser and he hardly had any spare time. I was so selfish.

"Don't mind Roger. He thinks he's funny."

Roger dished up a plate and passed it to his father.

"Don't believe anything that comes out of Roger's mouth. Liam is a big boy. and I'm pretty sure he knows what he's doing," his mother said. "So, Vivian, tell us about yourself."

"Well, there isn't too much to tell. I pretty much live at my restaurant and when I'm not, I'm playing volleyball or running."

Michael cleared his throat. "Any kids?"

"Nope, no kids for me. My sister lives with me right now. She has a little baby girl, Melody. It's just the three of us."

"In addition to owning her own business, she helps her sister raise her child. She's a saint," Michael said, patting my arm.

I helped myself to the rigatonis and passed the bowl to him with a nod of gratitude for his kind words.

"Olivia actually does more for me than I do for her. She cooks and cleans and keeps me sane. It's hard to get lonely with a sweet cuddly baby around."

Liam's mother poured us all a glass of wine. "Oh Dear, that's so true. Are you getting baby fever?"

"No. No babies in my future. I always tell my siblings I'd rather be an auntie than a mom."

Michael and Rose exchanged nervous glances with each other, leaving me feeling defensive.

"Don't get me wrong, I love children."

Rose put her hand up to stop me. "There's nothing wrong with not wanting to have children. This is such an uncertain time in the world, and you're obviously very busy. Liam works pretty hard himself. Running a business isn't easy."

"When he's actually at work. So, how long have the two of you been dating since Liam here never tells us anything," Roger said.

"We aren't dating, Roger. There's nothing to tell," Liam said.

"Oh, I see. My bad. The way you look at her suggests there's a story to tell."

Liam glared at his brother.

"Alright, Roger. Give your brother a break. You always know how to get him riled up." Rose looked at me. "Tell us about your family."

"Well, I have four sisters and a brother."

"Wow, that's a big family."

"Yeah, we aren't as close as we used to be. Growing up, we were much closer but then everyone kind of grew up and moved all over northern Minnesota." The truth was they moved because of the constant bickering between us siblings.

"That's too bad. I can tell you have a huge heart. I'm sure you'll all reunite soon. Your aura is very positive. I can feel it," Rose said.

I felt my cheeks flush. I'd never been great with taking compliments. "Thank you."

Once we finished eating, Rose stood up to take the plates, but Michael stopped her. "No, no. You cook and I clean. You know I'd never let you touch a dirty dish, but you never stop trying."

She smiled. "I don't deserve you, Michael. Thank you."

"Now go relax with our guest. I've got this." Michael turned to Roger. "Stay here, Roger. You'll be more use doing the dishes than causing trouble with our guest."

I pursed my lips to cover my smirk.

We sat in the living room, and Rose took the recliner in the center of the room. She jumped up. "I forgot dessert. I'll be right back."

Liam smiled at me as if he was right. Once she was out of the room, he leaned toward me. "Follow me."

He led the way up the stairs to a bedroom. The room was luxurious with soft, neutral tones of warm ivory and gentle gray. A textured throw lay at the foot of the bed. Matching nightstands and classic lamps with thoughtful proportion anchored the space.

A glass picture of the familiar Lake Superior beach with fine, black sand made from discarded taconite contrasted the breathtaking water of the familiar icy blue lake and rocky cliff. I smiled at the childhood memories the image brought back to me.

I pointed at the picture. "That's Black Beach in Silver Bay, isn't it?"

He walked over and stared at the picture with me.

"It is. My mother used to take Roger and me camping on Lake Superior in the summers. The North Shore was our very favorite place to hike, and Black Beach was my mother's favorite place to explore." He ran his fingers over the rocks. "I'd forgotten how beautiful it is over there."

"My sister Charlee lives on the Northshore."

"Oh, really. What does she do over there?"

"My parents own a resort and she helps manage it."

He nodded, an impressed expression on his face. "That sounds like a dream. Are you two close?"

I shook my head and my heart sank at the thought. "No, not anymore."

He changed the subject as if knowing I did not want to talk about it and walked over to his mother's dresser. "Come here. I want to show you something."

"Are you sure your mom won't be annoyed we're in her bedroom? I feel like we're crossing a line by being in here. Bedrooms are supposed to be—"

He lifted a beautiful wooden box off the top of the dresser and opened it in front of me. Inside were a bunch of folded up pieces of paper. It looked like rows of letters.

"My mom won't mind at all." He nodded at the box for me to take one.

I put my hand in the box and chose one of the folded-up pieces of paper. "You sure she won't care?"

He nodded and set the box on the table.

I unfolded the handwritten note dated February 20th, 2026. I looked up at Liam again for his consent to read it.

He nodded. "Go ahead, read it."

I cleared my throat.

*My Dearest Rose,*

*This morning, I awoke to the warmth of your body snuggled up to my side. Your snores were light and your face was as gorgeous as I've ever seen you. It is unbelievable how much more beautiful you get every single day. You age so gracefully, and I never thought I could love you more than I do, but every day our love continues to grow. I feel like the luckiest man alive to be able to wake up next to you every single day.*

*This morning I'm feeling so grateful to spend the day with my best friend and every single day for the rest of our lives. When I'm not here with you, I carry you in my heart. I look at our children and everything amazing we have accomplished over the years together, and I can't believe how lucky we are to have found our soul mates. I will never take a single day for granted because we never know when it will be our last.*

*I have set up a spa day for you and a friend at the Pebble Spa in Canal Park. Get yourself pampered because you deserve it. Thank you for all you do for our family. You are the rock that holds our family together.*

*Yours,*

*Michael*

I wiped my eyes, the stray tears refusing to stop flowing. I laughed through the tears and peeked in the box.

"Are these all letters to your mother from your father? There must be hundreds of them."

He took my hand and led me to the closet and opened the door. A hundred or so boxes were stacked up neatly.

My eyes widened. "Are those all from him?"

Liam shook his head. "Some boxes are letters my mom wrote to my dad."

"That's so beautiful. How long have they been doing this?"

He shut the closet door. "Since they started dating many years ago."

I stared in disbelief. After all these years, they still wrote each other love letters?

"I told them flowers were a lot easier."

I laughed and punched his shoulder. "You did not."

"You're right because he still sends her flowers, too."

"Okay, I think it's time for me to swallow my pride and say you're right here. True love really does exist even though I hate to admit it."

His arrogant smirk grew.

"Wipe the smile off your face, Liam. Just because it exists for them doesn't mean it exists for the rest of us. They are one in a million."

"You're a tough audience, you know that, Miss Vivian."

"So, this is where the two of you escaped to."

I turned to see his mother standing in the doorway, her hands on her hips. I dropped the box of notes, and they flew across the wooden floor.

I yelped. "I'm so sorry!"

I dropped to my knees to gather up the letters. This was it, she would hate me. Why did I let Liam talk me into reading an intimate letter not meant for my eyes. I wanted to disappear right into these walls. I could never face this family again.

# CHAPTER 12

## Liam

MY MOM SHOOK her head at me and dropped to her knees to help Vivian clean up the letters.

"Please don't tell me they're in order by date," Vivian said. "I'm so sorry. I'm such a klutz sometimes. This is going to take forever to put back in order. Please let me do it. It's all my fault." Her cheeks glowed red.

My mother took the box from her and tossed in the rest of the letters. "Don't you worry about it. Michael and I are very open about our love notes. I can organize them later. You're our guest. No harm done. Now, let's have some apple pie and forget about it, okay?"

My mother was open about her love for my father and their letters. She even had one framed in the bar area downstairs. She wanted Roger and I to open our hearts to love, even if we got our hearts crushed in the process, which I had many times. I was more of a romantic than Roger because I was comfortable in my own skin. Roger was a bit more macho. He liked to play the hard-to-get role with women. He had no problem getting women, but he struggled to keep them.

My father and Roger were still doing the dishes when we sat down at the kitchen table.

Mom dished Vivian up a piece of apple pie ala mode and placed it in front of her. She leaned in and whispered, "If you are wondering why we do the dishes by hand, we don't have a dishwasher. We're old fashioned like that. A little work never killed anyone."

I hid my snicker. My mother was taking a liking to Vivian and no wonder. Viv radiated kindness.

"Don't let her fool you, my parents love doing the dishes together. That's why they won't invest in a dishwasher," Roger said, coming up behind my mother and grabbing a plate of pie before sitting down next to Vivian. "Isn't that right, Ma?"

"I suppose so. How else would I get your father to listen to music and dance around the kitchen with me?"

"I'd drop everything and dance with you anytime," Michael said with a wink. He turned toward Vivian "How else would a guy like me keep a beautiful woman like this all these decades?"

Vivian's smile widened and she made eye contact with me. She had absolutely no clue what that smile did to my heart. How much everything she did affected me.

By the time we wrapped up the night and said our good-byes, Vivian had a permanent smile on her face. Nothing about it was fake or forced.

I ran ahead to open up her car door before she could protest. She smiled and shook her head at me. She was not used to being treated special. She should be. Any guy would be stupid not to treat her like a woman who deserved the world. I would do anything for this woman.

I put my hand on the shifter, and she put her hand on top of mine to stop me. I looked over at her.

"You win," she said.

"Win?" I said, confused.

"Your parents. That was true love if I ever saw it. I'm not saying I think it happens to most people, but with them I can feel it in everything they do for each other. I can see it in your father's eyes, your mothers smile." She stopped to pause. "How is it possible after all these years, they're still so in love? That they write love letters and respect each other."

"It's my normal. It's always been this way." I put the car in reverse and took off down the road. "I used to think everyone who was married lived like this. Then I grew up and realized marriage was hard work. It wasn't always this way, you know."

"What do you mean?"

"They had their hard time and struggles. It's not like they never fought, but they fought respectfully."

She eyed me curiously. "How so?"

"They never called each other names, and they never went to bed angry. They always kissed goodbye and good morning. They would listen to each other during arguments without disrupting or disrespecting each other. They didn't always do this, but their relationship just keeps getting stronger and stronger. My biological parents were the same way."

"That's beautiful. I've never seen anything like it. They're good people. You're really lucky, you know that? I love how they are both your parents to you. Them and your biological parents."

She put her hand on my leg and squeezed my thigh gently. "Thank you for inviting me here. Helping me believe love is possible."

Fear and willpower kept me from stopping the car and kissing her. She was so beautiful, but I knew I couldn't cross that line with her. I'd ruin the relationship we had, and I'd never have a chance with her. I needed to take it slow and hope she'd finally see me as more than a friend or an employee.

She pulled her hand away, and I wanted to grab her hand and hold it before it was out of my sight. Again, the willpower. "Now, back to reality. I just hope one day I can share a connection with someone like your parents do. My eyes are open now. Thank you."

"I'm so glad it helped."

"I also want to thank you for taking care of me the other night. I needed to relax and I let myself have one too many, but that was not me."

"Maybe that's a good thing. We all need to let loose sometimes. Don't be afraid to have a good time once in a while. You work so hard. You should enjoy yourself."

"See, this is why you're my person. You always know just what to say."

I only wish I did.

A pile of tax forms waited for me when I walked into my office. They needed to be completed before the April 15 deadline. I needed to step up or I would have to file way too many extensions. I was torn. I didn't want to take time off from the restaurant, but to keep my business running I needed to focus. I knew Vivian would understand, but I hated leaving her when she needed me the most. A little less sleep and a lot more work for a while as I focused on the bar and my business at the expense of my self-care. When tax season was over, everything would be better.

I woke up with my head on my desk, the sunshine poking in through my office window. Sleeping at my desk was becoming a normal occurrence The sun was a huge sign I'd overslept. How much? I picked up my phone. Eight o'clock.

"Shit," I said, jumping to my feet.

Although I had at least four hours of sleep last night, the most I'd had in a couple months, the exhaustion left me in a brain fog and a sense of disorientation. I splashed some water on my face in the bathroom. My reflection in the mirror told a gruesome story. I saw the bags under my red eyes and small wrinkles on my face. They were a small price to pay to keep Vivian's bar running and my clients happy with their tax results.

Time to call some of my clients. I used my charm to calm down angry clients who were not happy their taxes were taking longer than promised. My parents always said my superpower was my love for life and my ability to win almost anyone over. I connected with most personalities without even trying. I listened more and talked less.

Once my phone calls were completed, I collapsed at my desk and opened up the next file. I had nine hours before I needed to be at the bar. Time to get to work and stop wasting time thinking about everything on my plate. Once I saved my business and helped Vivian save hers, then I would sleep. If not, I could always sleep when I was dead, I suppose.

# CHAPTER 13

## *Vivian*

MY FEET POUNDED against the ice and pavement as I played over last night in my head. Rose and Michael, Liam, even Roger They were a real loving family and I felt so comfortable there. That love was refreshing, and I felt like I'd known them all my life. Hearing his parent's love story changed the whole recipe inside my soul. Their love was beautiful and inspiring. Although I now believed in love, I still did not think it was something I'd ever find. But good for them.

My lungs burned as the cold air crystalized with each inhale. I moved faster and harder. Thoughts of the fundraiser and everything I had to do to get ready for it weighed me down. Would a fundraiser even work? Was my situation hopeless? Maybe I should give in before I failed.

No, I had Liam and Alyssa and my sister to help me. I could do this. I had to try. If not, I'd always wonder if Liam's plan would have been successful. I could not let my negative thoughts stop me from fighting. I came to be a restaurant owner because I was a fighter. I'd worked my butt off to get where I am. Now was the time to fight even harder.

It didn't take long before I struggled with my balance, and

slipped on the ice and went flying to the ground. I landed in a snowbank and laughed. Was I hurt? I moved my arms, my legs, then I pushed up to my feet. My butt was a little sore, but nothing felt broken. As I walked, my butt felt a little better with each step.

Once inside my house, I changed and sat down to make a to do list for the fundraiser. I stared at the blank page. I knew nothing about putting on a fundraiser, who was I kidding? My front door opened.

"Vivian, you home?"

I got up from my seat at the breakfast bar. Olivia stood in the entranceway with Melody in her arms, both of them staring back at me.

"Give me that baby girl," I said, grabbing her from my sister. I cradled her in my arms and hugged her. I needed a baby to hug. Melody's snuggles fixed everything.

"What are you up to?" Olivia said. She picked up my notebook. "A fundraiser?"

I had to tell her at some point. "The guy who owns my building is selling it, so Liam convinced me to put on a fundraiser for a downpayment to buy the place."

"Sounds like a good idea. I love parties!"

I raised my eyebrows at her, and she put her hand on my shoulder.

"I'm sorry. I really am so sorry to hear that you're going through this, but at least we can have fun putting this fundraiser together. I have so many ideas."

I shook my head. Of course she did. Fundraisers were more Olivia's kind of thing than mine. I wanted to do this on my own, so I was not putting pressure on anyone else, but I needed her help, and I'd have to let my guard down. I had no choice if I wanted to keep my restaurant. "Okay, you can help."

She jumped up, "Yay! You won't regret this. Should I start a list?" She sat down at my spot.

"Go for it. Why don't you make the list while I give Melody a bath and we can touch base when I'm done."

"You're a saint, really. I'll grab a towel and her clothes. You have no idea how much I need this. I love being a stay-at-home mom but every day feels like the same routine. It will be fun having something to focus on again."

Melody's smiles in her tiny little tub were exactly the distraction I needed. Babies were the perfect remedy for all my stress and pain. I almost forgot for a few minutes about my situation. All I could think about was this tiny, sweet little girl with big blue eyes and the most adorable chubby cheeks.

I started off humming then sang all the baby songs I could remember from my childhood. Funny how I had forgotten so many songs I knew as a kid. But she was not judging me, so it didn't matter what I sang. So, I sang the newest Sabrina Carpenter song, and she cooed along with me, but at her own beat.

I washed her hair and then wrapped her up tight in her towel and carried her into the bedroom where the small space heater was on full blast and her clothes were all laid out. I talked in my baby voice to her until I heard someone clear their throat from behind me. I turned around. Liam was standing there with two Caribou Coffees in his hand, his eyebrows raised in an amused expression.

"Don't let me interrupt your cute baby talk."

I grabbed the pillow off the bed and threw it at him. He laughed and turned to the side so the pillow would hit him in the hip instead of his hands.

"You almost made me drop your coffee."

I held Melody to my chest and made my way past him to find my sister. "We both drink the same kind of coffee. Why would it be mine that you dropped?"

"Because I already drank out of mine, and I wouldn't want you to get any boy cooties."

"Oh, please. You're no boy." Okay, that came out wrong. I

could not take my words back but I really wanted to. Just as expected, I heard a laugh.

"Are you calling me a man?"

I ignored him and passed over Melody to her mother.

"Did you have a fun bath with Auntie Viv?"

Melody's little limbs flailed in excitement.

"She loves her auntie, don't you, sweet little pea?"

"I think they're best friends," Liam said. "Watch out for this one. I heard her plotting a kidnapping and Melody seemed excited to be her accomplice."

I gave him my best glare without smiling.

"Okay, I'll be nice. Here's your coffee."

I put my hand out. "Nope. I want the other one."

He put it behind his back. "Nope. I drank out of it."

"I don't care. How do I know you didn't poison mine?"

Olivia laughed. "She has a good point." She made her way to the couch to feed Melody.

"Fine," he said, handing the other cup over to me. "Why do I have a feeling you knew I would want the other one? Maybe you poisoned this one."

"Okay you two, stop flirting and let me read my list to you."

I sat down next to Olivia on the couch and Liam took the recliner across from us. Olivia picked up the notebook next to her and began reading.

"I think we should have a chili cook-off competition and a silent auction or maybe a band playing and some kind of theme for the event like a cool James Bond theme. I also think selling raffle tickets will bring in some cash. Not only would we make a killing on the alcohol, but people will buy off the menu, too."

I loved to hear the excitement in Olivia's voice.

"I think that's a great idea. I also think having food off the menu would be a good idea. We could attract people of all ages, too. Maybe family stuff and then have more of an adult event later in the night. What about having a craft table for the kids?" Liam said.

His ideas surprised me.

"Wow, Liam. That's a great idea," Olivia said and then turned to me. "Mom and Dad would pitch in to help with that."

"You and Mom could be in charge of the crafts. We could have the kids come earlier in the night, then just adults once the band starts." I said.

Olivia nodded, deep in thought. "That's a brilliant idea."

I squeezed her hand. "Thank you. Both of you." I said, turning to look at Liam. "We have a lot of planning ahead, but none of this would be possible without the two of you."

"It's my pleasure. Now, I better get to work." Liam turned to me. "Call if you need anything at all."

Once he was gone, Olivia's smile widened. "That man is so into you."

I rolled my eyes at her. "Here we go."

She shrugged. "What?"

I just shook my head at her. She knew exactly what.

# CHAPTER 14

## Liam

THE MORE I WORKED, the more I fell behind. At six in the evening I finally locked up. Roger was still in his office meeting with a client when I snuck out. I knew he'd give me crap for leaving, but I had finished up a lot of files during the day even if those curls and that laugh were never far from my thoughts. I was just about to hop in my car when I heard, "Liam, sneaking out already?"

I waved at my brother, but he moved fast and put me in a headlock.

"Rog, how old are you?" I said as I tried to pull his arm off me.

"About twelve."

He loosened his arm from around my neck after he messed up my hair with his knuckle a little more. "Let's get a drink, huh? Like the good ol' days?"

"I can't," I said, running my fingers through my hair.

"Come on, pretty boy. When was the last time you went out for a drink with your brother?"

"I can't, Roger. I have to work at the bar."

He jumped in front of me, blocking me from my car.

"You and I both know you don't need the money. You're

working day and night and hardly getting any sleep. This is definitely about that hot brunette, isn't it?"

I wanted to smack that grin right off his face. Sometimes he was such a pain in the butt. When would he ever grow up?

"I like being a bartender and yes, Vivian is a friend of mine. But nothing is going on with us, okay?"

He threw his hands up in surrender and stepped away from the car door. I stared at him, my suspicions alerted. He had given up too easily, but as I slid into my car, he stood back.

Roger walked into the bar and sat down in front of me. I knew my getaway was too easy.

He slapped a twenty on the bar. "Whiskey sour."

I stared into his eyes while blindly grabbing a lowball glass with one hand and the bottle of Jim Beam with the other. I topped the whiskey off with sour from the gun. My eyes never diverted from his face. His grin widened as I set the drink down in front of him.

"What do you want?"

"Can't a guy hang out at the bar with his brother and keep him company?" He sipped his drink. "Is the boss around today?"

I shook my head and went back to washing glasses beneath the bar. I would not answer his stupid questions. He was just trying to get a rise out of me.

"Look who decided to grace my bar with his presence. What an unpleasant surprise," Vivian said with a smirk as she made her way around the bar next to me. She looked over at me and back to Roger. "What did I walk into? The two of you don't look very happy. Everything okay?"

Neither one of us responded and a moment of awkward silence passed.

"I'll let the two of you continue whatever this is, but if you start getting scrapy I'll spray you both down," she said as she aimed the drink gun at us, the nozzle waving back and forth from him to me.

We both smirked. Behavior like that was why I fell hard for her. She was funny and kind and knew how to lighten the mood or break up a fight.

"Roger. Always a pleasure," she said with so much sarcasm I had to cover my smirk with my fist.

I followed her with my eyes as she disappeared into the back.

Roger cleared his throat, and I felt my cheeks heat up, but my actions were involuntary. I was incapable of stopping myself from watching her when she left a room. I thought I was discreet but obviously if first Alyssa and now Roger had picked up on my affection, I was terrible at hiding it.

"If you're going to sacrifice everything you have worked for on a piece of ass, you're an idiot. Does she even know how you feel?"

I stayed silent. Roger shook his head at me and grinned.

"Wipe that damn grin off your face or I will," I said, my finger just inches from his face. His smile widened.

"Wow, you really are into this girl. Aren't you?"

He was not about to leave, and I was going to lose my temper. The last thing I wanted was for a fight to break out between us here of all places. I was sleep deprived and on a short fuse. I had no patience for him today or the way he treated Vivian at dinner. "Grow up, Roger."

I grabbed a rack of clean glasses and carried them into the back room before I said or did something I would regret.

Vivian put her hand on my shoulder, startling me as I put the rack on the counter. "You okay?"

I nodded, staring at the ground, my hands in fists.

"Don't let him get to you. He loves getting under your skin. Surprise him and don't react to his words. Trust me."

She squeezed my shoulder before walking away.

She was right. As always. I closed my eyes and took in a deep breath and held it as I mentally prepared myself to face my brother again. Although we were close, sometimes he could be a cold-hearted jerk. My sister was the only one who could get him to listen and make him see he was being a prick.

I walked back to the bar and there was Vivian, her face just inches from Roger's surprised face.

"There's the big guy. Your girl here was just telling me about the fundraiser for the bar. I think we should bring the band back together to play. What do you think?"

I struggled to swallow the lump in my throat. The band. Was he serious?

Vivian's eyebrows pulled together. "What band?"

"Don't listen to him. We haven't played in years," I said.

She waved her finger between us. "You two were in a band?"

"Just a hobby band," I said.

Roger shook his head. "Oh, he's just being humble. Have you ever heard my brother sing?"

"No, I haven't." Her thoughts seemed to be spinning.

I let out a sigh. "It was years ago. I don't sing anymore."

How could Roger do this to me? He knew I hadn't played the guitar or sung for years. I had vowed I never would again.

Roger took another drink and slammed the empty glass back on the bar. "But don't you think this is the perfect time to get the band back together?"

He would not stop until I gave in. But not this time. "No."

"Who else was in your band?" Vivian said to no one in particular.

Roger leaned forward, excitement radiating through him. "A couple friends from high school, and Samantha. Right, bro?"

I turned around and avoided him. "There were six of us."

"They're all still around, and I bet they would love to play together again. You wouldn't want to let Vivian down, now, would you, brother? I'd play for free, and I bet the others would, too."

I stayed silent.

"It's for a good cause," Roger said. When I didn't respond, he added, "I guess he doesn't support your bar as much as you thought."

"Please, Liam. It would be fun," Vivian pleaded. She batted her eyelashes at me and pulled on my arm like a child.

Roger had begged me many times to get the band back together. So did the other band members, but it hurt too much to even think about playing and singing again. Roger knew why I quit singing, and he knew I would hate explaining the reason to Vivian. But he also knew I did not want to let her down. "You know what? I'm in." The words popped out of their own accord.

Rogers eyes bulged in his head. "What did you just say?" He hopped off his barstool and wrapped his arms around my head, once again messing up my hair with his fist.

"I'm going to change my mind if you don't take your damn hands off me."

My brother put up his hands in surrender. "I think I'll sneak out before you change your mind." He gave Vivian a quick nod before taking off out the back door. "Thanks for the support, Viv. You won't' regret this."

What in the hell did I just agree to?

# CHAPTER 15

## *Vivian*

SOMETHING WAS BOTHERING LIAM. He was angry at Roger for a reason and Roger had to push him hard to agree to join the band again. I knew Liam would do anything to help me, and I was the only reason he agreed. I needed to find out why.

"Everything okay? I didn't mean to push you into anything back there with your brother. I didn't know you played, and I have to admit, I can't wait to see you put on a performance."

"I'm okay," he said, avoiding my gaze.

Clearly he was not okay. "When was the last time you played?"

He hesitated, like the answer would hurt if he said it out loud.

"When I was sixteen."

"Sixteen?" I said. Before I could say anything else my heart stopped. "Wait a minute. That's when your parents passed. Isn't it?"

He finally looked at me. "Yes."

"Is that the reason you quit playing?"

He looked away again. "Yeah. My dad taught me how to play the guitar and the piano. He was at every gig, and he bought my equipment. He was even our band manager. I could never play again after I lost them."

"And here I am making you feel bad about not playing. I feel like such a jerk."

How did I miss this? I felt terrible for pushing him when he was not ready to play again.

"No. Not at all." He dug his fingers into his eyes. "I needed a little push. I've been thinking about playing again. I'm going to try. That's the best I can do. But I worry I won't be able to feel the music the way I used to."

I put my arms around his neck and gave him a soft hug, snuggling my head under his chin. "I'm so proud of you for saying yes. For putting yourself back out there. I may not have known your dad but one thing I know is he would have been so proud of you."

He nodded and forced a smile. "And if I suck?"

"I don't think that's possible. It's like riding a bike, right? You really don't forget."

"Maybe. I hope you're right."

I pulled my head away and looked up at him. He was so handsome I had to take a step back before I did something stupid. His lips were right there, and emotions were messing with my head and my heart. I played it off with a laugh. "I'm always right."

"That's true," he said.

If there wasn't any chemistry between us, why did I feel him watch me walk away?


Liam and I arrived at my place close to midnight. I had to wake up Olivia. She wanted to get a nap in, but she also insisted we should wake her when we got home so we could start planning the fundraiser.

I opened her door and heard her snoring away. I quietly shut the door and headed for the kitchen.

"I can't wake her. She's sound asleep. Melody wakes up a lot in the night. Olivia needs every moment of sleep."

"I get it. What do you want to do? Push this off until tomorrow?"

"No, let's put a tentative plan together then we can compare notes with my sister tomorrow. I pretty much know what she wants anyway."

He grabbed a bottle of whisky off the table and poured us both a small shot in a lowball glass.

I grinned. "Make yourself at home."

"Don't mind if I do."

I loved that he felt comfortable enough to open up my cupboards and fridge and help himself. I'd told him many times he was more than welcome. Not having to play hostess for him was nice. By the time I got home at night, I was exhausted, and I did not want to wait on anyone. He got that and me.

We toasted and clinked glasses then spent the next hour drinking and planning the fundraiser. Liam surprised me with all of his ideas. He was so creative.

A yawn escaped me. Time to shut it down. "I think we've a lot of great ideas here to think about. Thank you for coming over."

He nodded and stood up to leave.

I grabbed his arm, and he turned back to look at me with a confused expression on his face.

"I have a guilty conscience, and I want to apologize again for pressuring you to play for my fundraiser. I feel like you do so much already."

He cupped my cheek. I closed my eyes, and an electric current shot through my body. I opened my eyes, but the room was blurry. Liam had to be drunk, right? Would he kiss me? The moment was so intimate, and his touch felt so right.

"I want to play for you."

"What?"

He nervously pulled his hand away and ran it through his hair. I expected him to apologize next but instead he said, "Come to my office with me and let me play for you while I still have liquid courage."

He caught me off guard. How should I respond?. "You… want me to…go to your office with you right now?" I looked past him at my microwave. "At two o'clock in the morning?"

He glanced at the clock and then turned to me again. "Yes. It's now or never. Do you want to hear me play?"

"But we're drunk. How would we even get there?"

"I have my ways. Trust me. What do you say?"

"I say, let me grab my coat."


Of course Liam had a friend who was an Uber driver willing to wake up in the middle of the night just to drive us. I peeked at Liam's phone. He had Venmoed the driver a hundred dollars. That would do it. I'd drive someone a couple miles in the middle of the night for a hundred bucks.

Liam led the way into his downtown office in the ten-story U.S. Bank Building.

"I had no idea how huge this building was," I said as we stood in front of the elevator. "What floor is your office on?"

He pressed a button. "The ninth floor."

I stared at the door next to him. "Do you ever take the stairs?"

"I do. I never take the elevator to be honest."

"Oh really? Let's make a bet. I bet you can't beat me up to the ninth floor by taking the stairs."

He raised his eyebrows at me. "Is that a dare?"

No way he could beat me, not after he'd been drinking. "Yes."

Before I could say another word, he opened the public stairs door and was gone.

I waited impatiently for the elevator doors to open but it was taking forever. Maybe he knew the elevator was slow.

The door dinged and then opened. I dashed into the elevator and pressed button nine four times until I realized I needed to push the door close button, too.

Every floor dinged before it finally reached the top and stopped. "Come on," I said impatiently. I felt a bit dizzy, and my stomach was a little queasy. I was hunched over when the elevator door opened and there stood Liam, panting and leaning over, struggling to catch his breath.

"How did you beat me?"

He put his hand up to motion for me to give him a second. Then he put his hand on his chest.

"You okay? Should I call a doctor?"

I grabbed his hand and put it around my shoulder as we both wobbled a few steps to Suite 900, just across the hall. The sign on the wall said Century Link and Medica. "You must have really good Wi-Fi up here, huh?"

He shook his head at me and laughed. "Sure."

The carpet in his office was light blue and the furniture cherry oak. Just one picture, the Duluth Lakewalk in Canal Park hung on the wall The view was probably close to the same from the south side of the building.

"Why do you have a picture of Canal Park on your wall when it's just a few blocks from here?"

"Come here."

He led me into his office off to one side and over to the window. "I know it's hard to see since it's dark out, but this is a view of the hill going up. It's a nice view but nothing to really look at. Now, if you come over here," he said and led me to the next huge floor to ceiling window. "This is a nice view of the building across the street. This view isn't my favorite."

"Okay?"

"Well, if you go to the other side of the building and look out the window it's the perfect view of Lake Superior and Canal Park. A suite was not available this high up with a view of the lake so my brother and I leased this office space in the hopes of something else opening up with the perfect view. We decided to do minimal decorating until that day comes so we don't have too much to move or an excuse not to go."

"That sounds like way too much thinking for a view of the lake."

"From up here, it's not just a view. It's a whole experience. Next time you come up to my office it will be in the daylight so I can show you what it looks like from across the hall."

Was this his way of inviting me back again?

He picked up a guitar leaning against the wall in his office and sat down on the love seat. He spent a minute tuning up his guitar and then cleared his throat.

He began to play.

I recognized the tune and closed my eyes as he sang *Blackbird* by the Beatles. One of my favorite songs of all time. My skin broke out in goosebumps at the beauty in his voice. I opened my eyes to sneak a peek at his muscled arms as he flexed his hands on the guitar.

Was I attracted to Liam? Why did I feel this overwhelming urge to kiss him right now? I sat on my hands for self-control. I was too intoxicated to trust my actions.

Liam finished the song and pulled out a flask. He took a swig then threw it my way. I caught it and did the same. The whisky burned my throat as it went down.

He followed with *Tears in Heaven* by Eric Clapton. I knew instantly he was playing the song for his parents. A tear ran down his face and the emotion in his words gave me goosebumps. Within seconds, I was crying with him. He stopped playing and put his hands over his face to hide the tears. I took the strap off his shoulder and placed the guitar in its case then cradled his head against my chest.

I squatted down in front of him, so we were face to face and I was just a whisper away. Then I kissed him.

# CHAPTER 16

## Liam

WHAT STARTED off as a sweet kiss between two friends quickly turned into an all-out make-out session. Vivian climbed on my lap and straddled me. My hands slid beneath the back of her shirt, and I was about to unsnap her bra when she started laughing.

I stopped stone cold. Was she laughing at me? At us? "What's so funny?"

She stood up and covered her blushing face. "You totally seduced me," she said, her laughter getting louder.

"Me? You crawled on my lap. You were trying to get in my pants, boss."

She pushed me back, and I fell onto the couch. She thought this was hilarious.

She was still laughing. "Did you really call me your boss when I just stuck my tongue down your throat?"

I pointed in her face playfully. "See, you admit you stuck your tongue down my throat."

"I'm not sure if your band performing at my fundraiser is a great idea. Who knows what I'll do to you. Your performance was hot and left me with no self-control."

"Okay, I'm not canceling now."

She rolled her eyes. "Oh, stop."

I wanted to convince her I wasn't kidding. That I was so in love with her it hurt, but she did not feel the same. We were both a bit tipsy and our teasing got a little out of hand. I was certain we would never be more than friends. I knew her.

"Let's never speak of this, okay? My sister would love to hear all about us making out. She's been wanting me to ask you out since she met you at the bar."

I smiled and bit my tongue. Just another day of getting my heart broken by this breathtaking woman who would never reciprocate my feelings.

This was my opportunity to take a risk and find out how she really felt. "Oh, and what do you say?" I could hardly breathe as I waited for her answer.

"I told her you are like a brother to me and we don't feel that way about each other."

Ouch.

She gave me a sideways look. "Right?"

"You're a lot of things, Viv," I said, flipping her hair over her shoulder and getting a little closer. I still had some liquid courage, and I was going to take advantage of it, now or never. Like ripping off a Band-Aid. "You're my friend, my boss, my teammate, my confidant, but I also feel so much more."

Her eyes widened and her mouth dropped open. She stared off into the distance until I could not take the silence any longer.

"Please say something."

She put her hand over her eyes. "I always thought you were joking with your little comments."

"Little comments?" I said at a higher syllable. "That was me flirting. Hoping. Waiting."

Yep, she was rejecting me right here and now. I never expected my chest to hurt so much.

"Flirting?" she whispered, as if trying to remember every

comment I ever made to her. "That's not possible. How could I not see that? I'm so stupid."

"It's fine. I never should have said anything. It's inappropriate."

"No. I think we are both a little too intoxicated right now, and you don't know what you're saying. We're friends, Liam. I think I'm going to lay down. I'm exhausted.

I took her hand in mine and sat her down on the couch in my office. I grabbed a blanket out of the ottoman hidden in the corner and covered her as she curled up. I sat on the edge of the couch looking into her eyes as they closed and then opened again.

"I'm glad you were honest with me and told me the truth. Now I know. I just want to get one more thing out," I whispered.

She tried to speak, but I put my finger to her lips to stop her.

"Just let me say this, okay?"

She nodded.

"I had to tell you the way I feel. Now I can move on since you don't feel the same way. I hope this doesn't ruin our friendship. It may take some time and a little distance, but I have my list of things to do for the fundraiser and we're going to kill it. Don't think for a minute I'll let you down, but I do need to take some time to focus on my job during the week, but I'll be there for my shifts on the weekends, okay? We both know Alyssa will snatch up the shifts I can't make in a heartbeat."

She nodded but took my advice and stayed silent.

"Now, get some sleep. I'm heading to my brother's office to sleep on his couch." I leaned in to kiss her on the forehead, and she flashed me a sympathetic smile.

"Please don't do this, Liam. Don't walk away."

I knew right then my confession would change everything between us. We would be awkward and never the same as it used to be. But I had no choice. I had to tell her how I felt or I'd regret it forever.

The office door slammed and woke me. I jumped off the couch, my heart beating rapidly in my chest. I had to rest my hands on my knees just to recover.

"Hey brother," Roger said from the hallway. "You're actually working. What a surprise." He took a minute to find me and then crossed his arms at his office door. "Why did you sleep in my office when yours is right next door?"

"Vivian was sleeping on my couch, so I came in here. Wait, is she in there?"

"No, I checked there first."

I bowed my head. "Oh." She left because she did not want to face me after my stupid confession.

His eyebrows lifted and he smirked. "Is she still playing hard to get?"

I shook my head. "Don't even start."

"You look like shit, Liam. Were you two out drinking last night?"

I groaned. "I don't want to talk about it. I have a lot of work to do. Do you happen to have a Tylenol for my hangover?"

"Who do you think I am? Of course I do." He opened up his desk drawer and threw the whole bottle at me. I snapped the cap off and grabbed a bottle of water out of the fridge.

When was the last time I felt this terrible? Not only did I lose my best friend, but I was physically ill from the whisky. What happened to my decision not to make any impulsive decisions? I was careful not to do anything stupid or drink too much. I let my guard down last night, but it wouldn't happen again. Today I was going to focus on work and sober up, but first I needed a shower.

"Can I borrow your car?"

He threw the keys at me without another question. "Here you go. Are you actually going to work today?"

I'd had it with his comments. "What's your problem, Roger?"

He sat down at his desk, no longer making eye contact with me. "I don't have a problem, Liam."

"Yes, you do. This past year you've been a total jackass. You're rude and always making negative remarks about me and my work. The way you treated Vivian at Mom and Dad's house was uncalled for, even for you. And no matter what I do, I can't get you to back off. What is it?"

He crossed his arms. "Fine. You're the problem."

"Me?"

"Yeah, you have always been the problem. You think you're perfect and Mom and Dad believe you're the good kid. After your parents died, I opened up my bedroom and shared my space with you and all you ever did was overshadow me. Better at sports, better with women. As we got older, it became worse. Poor Liam lost his parents in a car crash. Be more like Liam, he believes in love. Always how much I should be more like you from everyone."

His voice escalated and his face got redder as he spoke. I kept quiet to let him vent. He seldom showed his feelings.

"Poor Vivian, she's losing her restaurant, and you have to save her. How about me? How about our business? While you're out there chasing tail and focusing on her business, ours is failing, and I'm sick of picking up your slack, okay? Either you're in it or you aren't. Put in your time, it's tax season. We're accountants. What the hell is wrong with you?"

I waited a minute to make sure he did not have anything else to add, then I said, "Are you done?"

He collapsed in his chair. "Yeah."

"I told Vivian I would only work at the restaurant on the weekends now. That I needed to focus on my work."

He gaped. "You did?"

"Yes, I did. You were right, by the way."

"I'm always right," he said. "Wait, about what?"

"I'm really into her. Too into her."

He grabbed a pen and started clicking it. "And? What are you going to do about it? Will you tell her?"

I looked down and sighed. "I already did. Last night."

"And?"

He clicked the pen even faster. I felt it deep in my bones. "Please stop clicking that pen. You're driving me crazy."

He stopped. "Well, what did she say?"

"She doesn't feel the same."

"Did she say that?"

Did she actually say that? "No, but she insinuated it."

He stood up and leaned on the front of his desk. "How did she do that exactly?"

"She said she didn't know I had feelings for her. That we were just friends."

"Ouch. Are you sure that was what she said? Maybe she meant she was scared to ruin your friendship if this didn't last."

I looked away. "You weren't there. You didn't hear her or see the way she reacted when I told her. She was almost embarrassed by my confession."

"Or maybe she was just in shock because she didn't know you had feelings, and she needs time to digest this. What did she say this morning?"

"Nothing. She was gone when I woke up. We just went through this, remember?"

He put his arm around my shoulder. "I may not be great with women, but from an outside perspective, one of two things is going on. She's trying to process her feelings for you or she doesn't want a romantic relationship with her co-worker."

"If that is the case, I'll quit working at her bar."

"You really are whipped, aren't you?"

I reached out to mess up his hair. Now I also needed a long hot shower to wash my damn feelings down the drain.

# CHAPTER 17
## *Vivian*

"I KNEW IT! I knew he had feelings for you. I hate to say I told you so, but I told you so!" Olivia jumped up and down like she won the lottery. Little did she know I was not going to do anything about it. I rolled my eyes at her. "Are you done yet?"

"Probably not. I'm so happy he finally told you. I could tell. I could totally tell. I did tell you so."

I collapsed on my bed with a loud grunt.

"Why are you so upset about this? He's nice and hot and confessed his love for you." Olivia hugged herself. "It's your love story."

"Okay, that is a bit overboard. He doesn't love me and this is no love story." Telling Olivia was a big mistake. I knew that now.

She stood there gloating at me. "He looooooves you. He loves you. He loves you."

"What are you in the ninth grade now?"

She jumped on the bed and sat down next to me. "I'm just so happy for you."

"I don't know how I feel about it yet, okay."

"How can you not be sure? He's perfect."

"Can we just let it go for now? I need some time to process this."

Olivia was struggling to understand why Liam's confession was not so simple. I'd bring up Troy to her, but that would just upset her. She hid her feelings about him because we both knew he was still hung up on his deceased wife. If she were to go after him the outcome would not be good. He might never be ready for a new romantic relationship. My sister was not second best, and I would not let her get her hopes up.

"Fine, but this isn't the end of this conversation," Olivia said. "I'm not sure what you're so scared of. You always choose the bad boys. You have since we were teenagers. Now you have a chance to choose a good guy. The right guy."

She was right. Why did I always choose the jerks? Jimmy was in and out of jail all the time. He treated me like crap and then he would apologize, and I'd forgive him. After Alyssa told me he was sleeping around and that he had slept with her roommate, I put a final end to our relationship. Then he stole that booze from me. We had broken up at least three times with months where we did not speak and I'd find someone new. Yet somehow, I'd end up back with him for another week or two.

"No, I haven't. You're overreacting."

"I'm not overreacting. C'mon. Jimmy threatened to kill himself if you broke up with him the last time. That isn't normal, Vivian. That's like some type of manipulation strategy and it's disgusting."

"He just has a bad temper, that's all."

She put her hands on her hips all dramatic. "Are you kidding me?" She raised her voice enough to show she was mad but not too much where she would wake Melody.

"What about the time he stole a bottle of liquor from the restaurant or the time he stole all the money in the till? How about when he refused to get out of bed on Christmas and we found out he had overdosed, and we had to call an ambulance. She had tears in her eyes. "Viv, he tried to make you stop talking to your family."

I never realized how much Jimmy's antics upset her. "He was a lot."

The angry look in her eyes was gone, replaced with a look of pity. "Look at your history, sweetie. He isn't even the worst of them."

"So I have terrible taste in men, okay? They always seem to find me, and I fall for them. That's why I'm writing off men altogether."

"No," she said with a sigh. "You choose these men, Viv. You're a strong woman with a big heart and not one selfish bone in your body. You're always donating and volunteering and you're my big sis. I've looked up to you my entire life. It's time you let yourself fall in love."

"So you're saying you don't look up to me anymore? Now I'm just a total failure?" I could hear the pout and poor me in my own voice. Was that who I was now? My eyes filled with tears, and Olivia wrapped me up in a giant hug.

"No, no. I'm definitely not saying that. I still look up to you and I always will. But I think you need to start believing you're worthy of a good man, and if you like Liam you need to stop being a baby about it and give him a chance or you might lose him."

She had a point, but I needed more time. I was scared. What if it didn't work out and we risked our friendship for nothing? "Sure, Liam is cute and kind and one of my best friends. Hell, I think I trust him more than I trust almost anyone. He's good looking and I'm attracted to him. But I don't know if I can see myself with him, you know. And I really don't want to lose his friendship if we didn't work out."

Olivia pulled away to look me in the eyes. She wiped my tears away. "I get it. You're scared. There is risk here. Maybe he isn't your person, and he's just a good-looking friend. That's okay, too. Just don't make this decision and turn him down without knowing for sure. You could regret it for the rest of your life."

I nodded. She made a good point. "I promise."

"Good, now let's make a list of supplies we need for the fundraiser to distract your brain. Is Alyssa making the posters and advertisement?"

"Yes. She's so artsy, I can't wait to see what she comes up with."

Olivia gave me one last squeeze on the arm and stood up. "No time to waste. Let's get to work."

We spent the next couple hours coming up with a shopping list, businesses to ask for donations, and decorating ideas that would not break the bank. We knew Mom would love to be a part of the arts and crafts, so I called her to discuss my ideas with her She was heading to Michaels that afternoon to start buying what we needed.

It takes a village and thank goodness I had one behind me. But I was not looking forward to seeing Liam. I worried it would be awkward between us, and I did not want to deal with hurt feelings or puppy love right now. He was coming in to work on Friday night, so I had two nights to work on my feelings.

Within two days, my sister and I had pretty much everything planned out and the flyer was perfect. Olivia did a fantastic job. She posted it on social media and even paid to put it in the *Duluth News Tribune*. A part of me felt a little sick over having a fundraiser to save the restaurant, but I needed to suck it up and stop feeling like a failure. This bar and restaurant meant a lot to so many people, both customers and staff. The restaurant was not a charity case. I was not a charity case.

Friday night came and Liam showed up right on time. He

flashed me a smile and got to work behind the bar. The restaurant had been slammed ever since the flyer was posted. We had so many phone calls and people stopping in to show their support and even business owners who came in to donate their time, money, and even their merchandise.

I had never realized our community was so supportive. I'd lived here my whole life, and I'd attended a few fundraisers, but this was the first one I was putting on. We had so many donations, from books from local authors, gift certificates, sweatshirts and t-shirts to quilts. We even received great deals on Vista Fleet which was a sightseeing, dinner and sunset cruise on Lake Superior and the Duluth Harbor.

Friday night was the busiest night so far. We ran out of ground beef for the hamburgers. I had to make a run to Super One grocery store at eight o'clock.

I walked past Liam. He had on a polo shirt. The top two buttons were undone, showing off just enough chest hair. He was easy on the eyes, and I struggled to take my eyes off him. He was confident and his smile was so genuine as he poured two to three drinks at a time. He gave the customers extra attention and was great at multitasking. Then his eyes caught me staring and I had to turn away fast, totally busted.

A huge drinking crowd filled the bar around ten and then a bus full of hungry women from a bachelorette party arrived not too long after. They were already drunk and drooling all over Liam. I even saw one woman slip him her phone number. Luckily that woman was not the bride. My face heated up as I watched it happen, and it took everything in me not to walk over and throw away that piece of paper with her phone number. Why did I care? We were not meant to be together. Maybe I was worried some woman would catch his attention, and he would end up quitting his job at the bar. That had to be what I was worried about. I kept a safe distance until one of the women hopped up on the bar to dance for Liam, and liability issues immediately popped into my head. Definitely not jealousy.

I ran over to tell her to get down but Liam beat me to it. He lifted her by the waist and plopped her on the floor. She put her hands around his neck and stared into his eyes. She was model gorgeous. Not the super skinny kind of model but the curvy and drop-dead gorgeous kind of woman with brown curls and perfect skin. Did she even know what a pimple was? Probably not.

Was this the type of woman he was into?

I had to walk away so I would stop letting it get to me. Why did I care? I needed to stop overthinking things. I was driving myself crazy. But wow did his butt look great in those black dress pants. His shirt was tight enough to see those muscles bulging beneath with every movement.

I let Alyssa go home early since she'd been covering Liam's shifts all week, and I moved behind the bar with him. We were in perfect rhythm like always. We worked fast and did not stop until right up to bar close at two in the morning. Liam called out last call, and our tip jar was overflowing. We had already dumped it at least four times, but it just kept refilling. My heart was full. I loved how everyone showed up when we needed our community support the most.

Liam walked women out to their cars, and I focused on cleaning the bar until he returned to fill the coolers. By the time we finally got the last person to leave, it was two-thirty. I shut and locked the door. Liam and I were all alone.

The awkward silence stretched on. Neither one of us knew what to say.

"We each made three hundred and fifty-two dollars in tips," he said, trying to hand me a stack of bills.

I shook my head. "I don't take tips but thank you."

"I thought you would say that so I'm donating the tips to the fundraiser instead."

"You keep them," I said.

He placed the bills on the bar and walked away.

I guess that was the end of the conversation. Good thing. I no longer had any fight left in me. "Thanks Liam."

He put his jacket on once he finished mopping the floor, and I grabbed my purse and jacket out of my office.

"Do you need a ride?" Liam asked.

I shook my head. "I drove tonight."

I saw the disappointment in his eyes.

"Sure. Can I walk you to your car?"

I missed his smile. He was struggling to have this conversation with me. That made two of us. This was on me. He put himself out there, and I needed to stand up to the plate before the awkwardness became our new normal.

"I'd appreciate it. Hey, Liam?"

"Yeah?"

"I want you to know I heard you the other night. I have my own struggles right now, and I was hoping you could give me a little time to think about everything. I was in shock. I had no idea how you felt and—"

"Whatever you need," he said coldly. "You ready?"

# CHAPTER 18

## Liam

YES, I'm a jerk. No, I did not handle that well and yes, I wanted to take it all back. I wanted to apologize for putting her in this position. I was not mad at her for not saying anything back or asking for more time. But I was embarrassed and acting like a child. I felt rejected. Where should I go from here? She needed time to think about what to say so she could reject me gently. I wanted her to get it over with and quit drawing this out so we could both move on. Instead, I was stuck waiting and trying not to think about her, but damn she was so hard to forget.

I turned my chair around and stared out the window at the steep Duluth hill. The roads were pretty clear, the snow pushed to the side since it had not snowed in a couple of weeks. A strong wind was blowing off Lake Superior, making it cold and miserable.

When I had a stressful day, I would spend my lunches walking the skywalk connecting the downtown buildings. On cold days like this, walking the skywalk provided the most beautiful view from up above the city and through the city buildings. We had three and a half miles of skywalks connected, so I always found a new place to explore. Some of the walks were separated so I had to go outside and brave the cold to hit another skywalk. Today I had one mission. To find Starbucks.

In the summertime, the six point two miles of the Duluth Lakewalk was where I spent my lunch breaks. One of the benefits of owning my own business meant I did not have to be in the office at a certain time unless I had an appointment. I worked late hours and usually got to work before the sun rose this time of year. Except this year I had not prioritized my business because my heart was somewhere else. I wanted to see the Zenith Bar & Grill succeed.

I'd spent the last two days putting my head down and working hard to catch up. Roger was not wrong, I was letting my work slip and that was not okay. Only a few more weeks and tax season would be over, and I'd be able to breathe.

I got myself a coffee at Starbucks. After a couple wrong turns, I made my way back to the office. I stopped to look out the window at the beautiful lake in the distance. The *William H. Irving* was straight ahead and even from up here the boat looked gigantic.

"Liam?"

I turned around to find Olivia standing behind me, pushing a stroller. "Hi Olivia, what are you doing here?"

She bent over to check on Melody and put the pacifier back in her mouth. "I had to get Melody out for a walk, but it's too cold outside. That wind is horrible and takes her poor breath away, so I came in here to walk."

I took another sip of my coffee. I wanted to ask her about Vivian, but I needed to let it go.

Olivia smiled and a look of concern crossed her expression. "Where are you headed?"

"Back to my office."

"Mind if we join you?"

"I'd love the company. As long as if Melody wakes up, I get to pick her up."

"Deal."

We walked side-by-side down the hallway. The lunch crowd was dying off so the skywalk was not as congested.

"Have you talked to Vivian at all?" she said

Smooth. "No, we haven't spoken yet, but I'm working tonight so I'm sure we'll have to talk at some point."

"I know my sister can be a bit closed off, and she doesn't believe in love, but I want you to know I see the way she looks at you, and I know she feels the same way. She's just scared."

I wiped the sweat off my forehead with the back of my hand. "Yeah, I'm not sure she does. But I appreciate the kind words."

"No, really. Do you know why she's so afraid?"

I shook my head.

"She was in a long-term relationship with her high school sweetheart. They were inseparable. They did everything together and then one night she couldn't get a hold of him. His phone kept going to voicemail, so she drove over to his house and found him in bed with someone else."

"Oh no. How old were they? She never told me."

"She was twenty-three. She had just graduated from business school, and he was, well, celebrating her graduation without her, I guess."

"Where is this guy now?"

"Cade? I'm not really sure. I don't think Viv has seen him since then. He begged her to take him back, but she was heartbroken. She stopped believing in love and trusting men. Stayed away from the good ones for fear of falling in love again."

That explained a lot. She had her heart broken in the worst way possible, and she had stopped believing true love exists.

I needed to convince her otherwise if I ever wanted to have a relationship with her. "I wish she would've told me." Maybe I should have asked more questions.

"She doesn't tell anyone. She hates to even think about it. She'd kill me for telling you, but you needed to know it's not you. She's screwed up from it. Then what Ben did to me didn't help. She had started to believe what Ben and I had was real. Hell, he could have fooled me. I never knew what we had was one-sided."

Anxiety and anger pulsated through my veins. Guys like that never had a conscience. They made the rest of us good guys look bad. "There are jerks out there and sometimes they come off as the good guys because they're good at the game. Now she doesn't believe true love exists for her. She thought people just settled." It still broke my heart to think she really believed that.

"Yeah. She's quite the skeptic when it comes to love. She's been burned too many times. And I never saw how broken my relationship with Ben was until he asked me for a divorce."

"I dated a woman who broke my heart, too. It isn't easy. I hate that this happened to both you and Vivian. It isn't right. Those men were cowards."

She looked close to tears. I led her to my office, and she sat down on the couch.

"Don't give up hope with her. She'll see that true love exists. Trust me," Olivia said.

She placed her hand on my arm in a calming way. "Just be yourself. I know she wants to be with you. I can see it in the way she looks at you and the way she acts around you. That night at the bar she was so jealous of that woman talking to you. Just don't give up on her, okay? She's stubborn."

I nodded. "She's worth the battle but she's stubborn."

Olivia stood up and checked on Melody, who was peacefully sleeping in the stroller. "That's exactly what I wanted to hear. Now go get your girl."

I stood up, pacing back and forth in my office, the same question running through my head. How?

"But first, could you help me put Melody in my car?"

I laughed. "Of course."

# CHAPTER 19

## *Vivian*

I WALKED into my restaurant around five. After spending the morning and afternoon shopping for the fundraiser, I had to take a nap before I could even try to run my business. With Liam not working during the weekdays, Alyssa had stepped up, but I also had to step up. I had no idea how much work this fundraiser would be.

I snuck past Alyssa and Liam and went straight to my office. They were both underneath a table, trying to stop it from wobbling. I shut the door to my office and set everything on my desk before crashing onto the chair. With my thumb and middle finger squeezing the bridge of my nose, I focused on my breathing. I was unsure of how to act toward Liam. Was he mad at me? Was our friendship over?

I heard a knock and then Liam poked his head into my office. "You here?"

I put my hands down and sat up straighter. "Come in."

He opened the door wider so he could slip inside and closed it behind him. A sure sign this was not business related. My heart was ready to beat out of my chest at the anticipation.

"I wanted to see you before we started work. Well, together anyway." His cheeks flushed and he looked down.

Had I ever seen Liam blush? Not even when drunk customers slapped his butt or made forward remarks. Was I making him as uncomfortable as he was me? So much was riding on how this conversation went. Was he going to quit? Put in his two weeks? If he did, I might as well cancel the fundraiser right now.

He sat down next to my desk. "I never should have confessed my feelings for you like that."

I waved him off. "No, don't apologize for that. I should apologize for being such a coward, really."

He shook his head and smiled. How did I forget how sexy he was? That grin took my damn breath away.

"Now you're just being silly."

"No. I mixed business with pleasure. And I should have told you a long time ago that I needed time off to focus on tax season. I offered to help you and then pulled away. I'm sorry. I don't process rejection well."

"You have nothing to apologize for. I know you, and I should have known you needed some time off to focus on your business right now. It's just that you're my best employee, and I was being selfish. I should have thought more about you instead of letting my business failure take over."

"Business? You really think I believe you only have professional feelings for me? You and I both know there is more."

He stood up and I followed. He took a couple steps toward the door, and I jumped in front of him.

Once he placed his hand on the doorknob, I yelled out, "Liam, please stop!"

Now what?

He turned around and looked at me with a confused expression on his face. "Everything okay?"

I shook my head. "No." And without thinking, I let down my guard and crashed my lips against his.

I felt his body tense at first, before he relaxed and pulled me toward him with his strong arms. He pushed my back to the wall with need and took my breath away.

For the next five seconds, I let myself fall. I only thought about his soft lips and the delicious taste of his mouth. Then out of nowhere, my anxiety started in my chest and ran through my core. I jumped back as if on fire. "I'm sorry. I just…"

He put a finger to his swollen lips. "Don't say anything right now, Viv. That kiss was long overdue. I'm not going to rush you, and I don't want you to say anything right now. Take your time to think, just don't overthink us, okay? You know me. You can't fight what we have."

He took a step toward me, my body too frozen to move. He gave me a slow peck on the lips, nothing near the way I devoured his mouth just a minute ago. His kiss was short and sweet, a tenderness I'd never felt before. He pulled away and stared at me, just inches from my face.

"We're good here. Just take your time. I'm not going anywhere," he whispered.

He looked back at me and flashed one last irresistible smile, and my heart fluttered.

I wanted to chase him down, call out his name again, and have sex with him right here in my office, maybe even on my desk. The image of him sweeping everything off my desk and onto the floor with a bang had my body overheating.

But another part of me wanted to run away. Instead, I took my boots off and slipped on my work shoes then went to help the kitchen prepare for the dinner rush.

I'd overthink this later. I always did. But right now I had work to do.

·  ·  ·

Alyssa left early, and by ten the kitchen was closed down, which left just Liam and me to work the bar. We were slammed so no time for small talk or awkward moments. I never noticed how bad my feet hurt until we were down to two people at the bar and I sat down to count the register. Liam was busy refilling the cooler when I followed the last two customers out.

I made my way to my office and walked right into a hard, bare chest.

Liam was standing there with his shirt off, another one in his hand.

"I'm sorry, I was trying to change my sweaty shirt from all the running around."

I struggled to speak. I was short, and his hard pecs and firm abs stared me right in the face. It took everything I had not to reach out and squeeze his muscles. The sweat glistened off his chest and damn he was hot.

He pulled his shirt over his head while I stood there, staring at him. I had no control over my body.

"Are you ok? Viv? You're staring."

I shook my head, as if to shake away the image of his bare chest playing on repeat in my mind. "I'm so sorry. I wasn't expecting to find you half naked."

His big belly laugh made me blush.

"I wasn't half naked. You've seen me with my shirt off before when I had that beer spilled on me a few weeks ago.

I never really looked at him or stared at him then. A hot flush rose up my neck. I pushed past him into my office and shut the door. I leaned against the door and covered my face with my hands. I wanted a do over of the last couple of hours. Pretend they never happened.

I heard a knock at my office door, and I exhaled. I had to face him at some point. I opened the door, surprised to see Jimmy standing there.

I stepped back, not able to get far enough away from him. "Jimmy, what are you doing here?"

"The front door was open. I thought I'd come in and see if you wanted a ride home."

Did he not listen? "No, Jimmy. We're over. I told you that. I don't know why you're here. You need to go. The door was supposed to be locked. We're closed."

Every step he took toward me felt deliberate, measured, like he was closing a distance I desperately needed to keep feeling even the smallest bit safe. The back of my legs brushed against my desk and left me knowing I had nowhere to go. I reached back to grab anything with weight in case I needed to fend him off. His eyes looked darker than I ever saw them.

I needed backup. "Liam!" I screamed at the top of my lungs, my voice cracking.

Jimmy grabbed me by the arms and pivoted to push me up against the wall.

"Why do you need Liam? I thought maybe you would come over to my place and we could have some fun," he said against my ear. The warmth of his breath on my ear made me shiver.

I moved my head to the side to avoid his lips, but he grabbed my hands and held them against the wall on each side of my head. His face in front of me, he spoke, almost hissed, through his teeth. The anger was enough to send chills down my spine.

"Let me go, Jimmy. Please, let me go," I said, hoping he was somewhat reasonable at the moment.

"What? You don't want me now? You little slut. Is there someone else?"

What did I ever find attractive about this guy anyway?

He dropped my hand and slapped me as I fought to get away. I cried out.

The door burst open, and Jimmy was yanked away from me.

I backed myself into the corner and peeked through my fingers at Liam struggling to pull Jimmy out of the office in a headlock. I grabbed the stapler off my desk and held it at the ready behind my back just in case. Liam finally pulled Jimmy out and I followed but kept my distance from them. Once we reached the front door of my restaurant, Liam threw Jimmy out into the street.

"You aren't welcome here. You come anywhere near her again and it'll be a lot worse next time. You hear me."

If Jimmy responded, I did not hear it. I shut the door as quick as I could behind Liam and locked it.

"Are you okay?" Liam's hands were behind my head as I cried into his chest.

"I don't think I've ever been so scared in my life. He's not normally like that, really."

"Shush, it's okay. I'm here. I'm never going to let anything happen to you."

And I believed him.

# CHAPTER 20
## Liam

"I DON'T KNOW what he would've done if you hadn't shown up."

"Shhhh," I said. Her body shook in my arms. "It's okay. He's gone now. This will never happen again. I can promise you that."

Her body relaxed in my arms. What if I hadn't been here? I needed to teach that guy a lesson and make sure this never happened again.

"Are you sure you don't mind staying over tonight?" Vivian kept asking me the same question.

"For the tenth time, Vivian, I'm staying." I had so much work to do but I could not leave Vivian. Not like this.

She was still a little shaky, so I insisted on staying over.

"There's nowhere I'd rather be."

She smiled shyly at me. "I'm going to take a shower."

"Are you sure you don't want to file a police report?"

If she did not report Jimmy, he might keep harassing her, but I didn't want to push and risk upsetting her even more.

"There's nothing to report. He didn't t do anything or even technically threaten me. Like I said, I'll fill out the paperwork for a restraining order first thing in the morning, but I don't want to deal with all that tonight. There just isn't enough to say."

"Okay."

She wrapped her arms around herself. "Do you mind if I jump in the shower?"

I shook my head and made my way over to her stove. "Do you have any tea in here? Some without caffeine?"

"Top shelf above the oven."

I found it in the first cupboard I opened.

For the next twenty minutes all I could think about was what would have happened if I had not heard her call out my name. If I'd only been there faster. Why did I leave her alone, and how did I miss that door not being locked? I put her in danger's way. She could have been hurt or killed or worse.

I searched for blankets for the couch. I went into her room to take the one off the end of the bed and when I turned around, she was standing in the doorway with just a towel around her. My body reacted and I let out a loud sigh.

"Liam, what are you doing?"

I kept my eyes locked with hers. "Sorry about that. I needed a blanket for a bed on the couch."

She moved quickly and put out her hand to stop me. "No, no, no. Please, sleep in here. I don't want to be alone tonight, okay?"

I nodded. I'm not sure I would survive a night alone with her in her bedroom without going crazy, but if she wanted me in here, I would stay. Even if every second I spent alone with her I was struggling with self-control, I would stay because she needed me.

She walked closer to me. Did she know she was killing me? She had nothing on under that towel. The thought made knots in my stomach.

"You're sweating. Are you sure you're okay?" she said.

What could I say to her? Her naked body was making me crazy, but I held back. Instead, I said, "I'm fine. It's just a little warm in here."

She twirled her hair nervously with one hand, her other hand holding the towel.

"Would it be too much to ask for you to sleep in bed with me?"

Oh no. How could she not see she was killing me? "Yeah. I mean, if you want me to."

She nodded. "Thanks, Liam. I appreciate it. I really hope I'm not putting you out."

"Not at all."

She grabbed some clothes and walked back into the bathroom. I left my T-shirt and underwear on and climbed into her bed.

She came out a few minutes later in a long T-shirt and possibly shorts underneath. Tell I had to believe she had something on under that T-shirt.

She had her back to me as she brushed and braided her hair while talking to me as if it was the simplest thing to do. How did she know her hair was perfectly weaved together?

"I really hope it isn't too much to ask for you to stay with me. I just know I won't be able to sleep if you aren't here with me."

"It's not a problem. I don't mind," I said. "Wait, I'm not on your side of the bed, am I?"

"Nope. I always like to be closest to the door," she said, pulling the comforter down on the other side.

She crawled into bed next to me. We were both on our backs. No sleep for me tonight. I would be wide awake wondering what was under her shirt. My mind was in the gutter when she needed me to be there to calm her down. I needed to do better and stop thinking naughty thoughts at a time like this.

Vivian cleared her throat. "Liam, I have a question for you."

"Okay."

"It may seem a little strange, but I know I won't be able to sleep if I don't ask."

Well, now she really had my attention.

"You didn't know you would be sleeping here, and I didn't see you carry in a bag, so what are you sleeping in?"

Was she playing me or just as curious as I was? Maybe she was as into my body as I was hers.

"You're correct. I had this white T-shirt under my sweater so I'm wearing that with a pair of underwear."

The air got quiet. Enough to hear a pin drop.

"Hey, Liam."

I blinked, staring into the darkness. "Yeah."

"What kind of underwear do you have on?"

I started laughing and couldn't control myself. The more I tried to stop, the harder I laughed.

She took her pillow, got to her knees and started hitting me in the face. I sat up and played tug of war with the pillow.

We both stopped.

My eyes adjusted to the darkness, and I could see a shaded version of her face. We were a couple inches from each other's faces.

She cleared her throat, and it woke me from a trans state. We laid down on our backs again.

"I'm wearing boxer briefs," I whispered into the darkness.

She let out a groan and rolled to face away from me.

After another minute of silence, I whispered, "Hey, Viv." She didn't answer so I continued. "What are you wearing under your T-shirt."

"Nothing," she said.

My eyes opened wide, and I laid there holding my breath. Did she just say nothing?

A torturous minute later, she started laughing and I rolled

away, punching my pillow. "You're an evil woman, you know that?"

"Goodnight, Liam."

"Goodnight, Vivian."

I would not get a bit of sleep tonight, that's all I knew.

# CHAPTER 21
## *Vivian*

A COUPLE SNORTS woke me up, and it took me a minute to realize who was lying next to me.

When he snorted, he half woke himself up, so he turned onto his side and wrapped his leg around my hip. A whole lot was going on down there.

I carefully removed his leg and set it down then slowly rolled out of bed, doing my best not to shake the bed. I had to admit, the snort was kind of cute, but I would never tell him that.

I slept so well with Liam beside me. He snuggled with me most of the night, and I felt safe.

I threw on my robe and headed downstairs.

Olivia was feeding Melody on the couch while watching *Good Morning Northland*.

"Good morning," she said as I walked past the living room and into the kitchen.

She got off the couch, still cradling Melody under a blanket and followed me into the kitchen. "So, how did everything go with you and Liam last night."

I sighed.

"That bad, huh? Did you guys at least talk."

"We talked." And we kissed and he saved my life. And then I took him home and made him sleep in bed with me. I even felt his excitement in his dreams. How did the last twelve hours change so much?

"Talked?" Olivia said in an unbelieving tone. "You talked? Did you at least hear him out? Maybe figure out you have feelings for him in return?"

I looked behind me to make sure he was not in the kitchen. She would find out he spent the night eventually, and she'd be really confused, then jump to conclusions. I opened my mouth to explain but she beat me to it.

"I see the way you look at him, Viv. You're in love with him. I see you eyeing him up, and I can tell this isn't a one-way street."

"Of course I stare at him, have you seen the man? He's gorgeous—"

A deep voice cleared his throat behind me, and my mouth dropped open. Liam was leaning against the kitchen entryway and grinning at me.

"I'm gorgeous, huh?"

A naked chest stared back at me. I snapped myself out of it. "Put a shirt on, would you?"

Olivia pointed back and forth between us. "Oh my gosh. No way. Did the two of you--" She cleared her throat, a giant grin spreading across her face. "It's a good thing Melody has this blanket over her eyes. This is no longer PG. I have to admit, you two surprised me."

She stood and filled a coffee cup with coffee. "I'll leave you two to it. Viv, I'll be in my room for the recap after he leaves." She smiled brightly and waved to Liam. "Liam, you stud." She winked and walked away before either one of us had a chance to reply.

I turned away from him and bowed my head to hide my flushed cheeks.

"I can only imagine what she's thinking we did. I'm glad I didn't put a shirt on," Liam said with a laugh.

He walked around me and whispered in my ear, "Gorgeous, huh?"

He poured a cup of coffee and grabbed an apple on the counter, leaving a chill that zipped its way down my entire body.

This was so bad. What did I get myself into? He was joking with me and had no idea the effect he had on me. At this point, I was sure any attractive man would have the same effect on me since I hadn't had male contact in who knows how long. Since Jimmy. The thought of Jimmy turned my stomach in knots. I should have known better than to date someone like him. Although I never thought it would work out between us, I never thought he would be so mean.

"Oh, shush. You know you're good looking."

This only made him grin wider, then his expression turned serious.

"How are you doing today? You slept well. You hardly even moved all night."

How did he know that? Did he stay awake most of the night? "I did. Thank you for staying with me."

"Whatever you need." He put his shirt on. "You know my number if you need anything at all, okay?" He headed back into my bedroom and came out carrying his jacket.

He was so genuine. I knew he would do anything for me. I never wanted to lose him. If we dated and I lost him, I'd lose everything. Too risky. He was my person. If only he could see it.

I nodded and smiled. "I will."

He left and not even five seconds later Olivia popped her head out of her room and loudly whispered, "Is he gone?"

"Yes, nosey."

She laughed and closed the door quietly, the baby monitor in her hand. "Okay, spill the tea."

I started putting away dishes that had been sitting in the strainer for two days. "I don't know what you're talking about.

She stood in between me and the dishes. "Oh, no you don't. I want to hear everything."

I peeked around her and grabbed another dish. "Excuse me."

"You don't just stand here and act like everything is fine. I felt the sexual tension. I know you didn't have sex, but he did come out of your bedroom without a shirt on. Start explaining or I'll corner him at your bar." She tapped her toe and crossed her arms.

"Fine." I took my time answering, just to mess with her. "It's really not as exciting as it sounds."

"Try me."

I stacked the two plates in the cupboard and sat down at the kitchen table. "Get us both a cup of coffee. Don't forget I warned you this isn't what you want to hear."

"Black coffee?"

I nodded. "Please. So, last night after everyone left, I went into my office and Jimmy showed up. I don't know how he got in."

"Jimmy?" She wrinkled her brow. "Why was Jimmy there?"

I shrugged my shoulders. "He got pissed at me and held my arms above my head. I called out for Liam, and he came before Jimmy could do anything."

She held my hands in hers. "I'm so sorry. Are you okay?"

"I'm fine. He just scared me, that's all. I didn't know what he was going to do. He's never done anything like that before."

"Did you call the police?"

"No, but I told Liam I would file a restraining order today, but I'm not sure I'm going to. The police would be no help. I had no evidence, it's my word against his."

"But the incident would be on file. That's the thing. If he did this again there would be a prior. I bet it would be a lot easier to get a restraining order if you had a police report."

She was right. I never thought about it that way. I was in shock last night and not thinking clearly. "That's probably true, but I just wanted to get out of there. I wanted to go home and sleep in my own bed. I really don't want to file one. I just want to forget this all happened. It's like a bad nightmare."

"Please think about it. Okay?"

I nodded.

"So, on another note, Liam volunteered to stay in your room with you?"

"He was a gentleman. I asked him to stay with me. I asked him to sleep in my bed. I trust him. He's my friend."

She snort- laughed. "Your friend, huh? When will you realize you two are way more than that."

"Drop it, Olivia. This is not the time."

"Listen," she said, leaning forward. "I always have your best interests at heart and if Jimmy ever comes around you, I'll kick his butt."

"You?"

"Yes, me. I'm not afraid to use some moves on him. Make him scared for his life."

I laughed. My sister did not have a fighting bone in her body. Although, when it came to people in her circle, I could see her fighting. Especially if she was worried about Melody getting hurt.

"Do you think he'll try to come here and see you?"

I shook my head. "I don't think he's that stupid. He was drunk and impulsive. He wasn't himself."

"Stop making excuses for him. Be careful, okay?"

"Okay."

"And Viv."

I glanced up at her.

"Don't let this one slip away. Whatever you decide, I'm on your side. But if you let him go, you may regret it for the rest of your life."

The truth was, I knew she was right.

# CHAPTER 22

## Liam

THE BAND WAS BACK TOGETHER for the first time in years. We got in a few practices virtually and a couple in person over the last week leading up to the fundraiser, and we sounded pretty good. We were short of time, but we stuck with most of the old songs we played together years ago and just added a couple new ones. I tried not to think about all the work on my desk at the office. The fundraiser was coming up fast and I struggled to be in two places at once. My voicemail was full of angry clients wondering when they could book an appointment for their taxes or wondering why they hadn't heard from me regarding taxes they needed completed. I was drowning.

Fundraiser day had finally arrived. An hour before the fundraiser was to begin, Vivian walked in as I was finishing the last place setting at a table. The fundraiser had a James Bond theme, and she was dressed in the most gorgeous black cocktail dress. Her brown curls were teased into a French role at the back of her head. Quarter size fake diamonds dangled from her ears. Her skin glittered and her smile widened the minute she saw me.

Her heels must have given her an extra two inches as she gave me a gentle hug and a kiss on the cheek.

"Liam, you look so handsome in a three-piece suit. I'm impressed."

She didn't add a comment about my gelled hair, which I would never admit I spent hours watching YouTube videos to perfect.

I looked around at the red curtains that hung on the wall, A 007 life size standee displayed in the corner, and a Bond Girls life size standee stationed right next to the martini bar. "Where did you get all this stuff?"

She smiled. "I have my ways." She leaned closer and whispered, "My mom went a little crazy."

"I'd say. This is every man's dream," I said, spinning around to take it all in.

Vivian fixed herself a martini and curled her finger. " Follow me."

We headed to the backroom where tables were set up for poker. A black carpet with the famous numbers on it covered the cement floor.

"This is unbelievable. I don't even know where you would find something like this."

She took a sip of the martini. "You don't know my mother. It doesn't matter how sick she is, that girl can shop."

She had mentioned her parents were not in the best of health but never elaborated. I wanted to ask her, but I let it go. She would tell me when she was ready.

"Are you all ready to pump everyone up with your band?"

"Let's just hope we are on tonight. We've been practicing a lot but we still aren't where we used to be."

She winked at me. "I'm sure you'll do great," she said as we made our way back to the bar

Alyssa waved at me from behind the bar. She was messing with the stereo and called out to me, "Hey, big guy!"

Vivian nodded toward Alyssa. "She must be setting up the playlist for the evening."

"Yes, she is. What's she playing? *Live and Let Die, Goldfinger*?" I said.

Vivian grinned. "*You Only Live Twice*, yep. All of the above."

"Well, you'll be surprised to hear I've been working on playing the Bond music tune on my guitar to start off the evening."

"I'm impressed. Let me show you something funny."

She led me over to a table. The ice buckets lit up and changed colors. "I love that. It's beautiful and lights up the whole room."

She paralyzed me when she reached up and straightened my bowtie, sending shivers down my spine at her touch.

"There, now you look perfect, James." Our eyes met and I had a hard time looking away.

I wanted to kiss that lipstick right off her face. Instead, I turned around and made my escape to test the speakers. Breathe, Liam, just breathe.

Alyssa hip-checked me and whispered, "If you're James Bond, she's your Bond girl."

I shook my head. I was not the one who needed convincing.

A couple barrels sat in the corner. I pointed to them. "What are those for?"

Alyssa led the way. "Diamond Digging. Olivia set this up. You pay fifty dollars to get an entry and then you dig for one of these balls." She pulled one out of the barrel and handed it to me. "They crack it open and find a fake gem or gift cards inside." She pointed to a collection of baskets. "The gems coordinate with those baskets up there to win prizes. Viv's family outdid themselves. If the people come, we'll have a great fundraiser. That I can promise."

"This is so much better than the chili cook-off idea," I said.

Vivian introduced me to her parents and I helped show them what they would be doing tonight. Her mother was excited to meet me and she was very vocal about how handsome she thought I was. Her father was a little more quiet.

My band showed up a few minutes early. Then the crowd moved in, and the placed filled up.

I started our set with the James Bond theme song on my guitar and then we went right into our old music. We were two songs in when I saw Vivian standing in the back of the restaurant watching me. Our eyes met, and she smiled before taking an order at a small table.

Samantha, my ex-girlfriend and old band member, winked at me. I wanted to say something to her, but I just needed to get through this fundraiser. I could tell she was into me, and we had yet to speak about our past or our present situation.

My voice held up and the crowd responded. The auctions for four tickets to the Duluth Playhouse and a three day stay at the Edgewater Hotel ended up being auctioned off for a couple hundred dollars. And the tickets for the raffle for the trip to Hawaii was overflowing, as expected. Tim and Lizzy got Pine Beach Resort in Side Lake to donate a cabin for the Fourth of July weekend, and Bimbo's donated $100 gift card and a couple sweatshirts. Olivia did a great job talking up their pizza and wings and the bidding got competitive quickly.

The poker game was intense. I watched the action between sets. Vivian's father was one of the dealers. He had quick hands and was the biggest winner at the table. My brother seemed to be the one losing all his money. I was glad he didn't know the dealer was Vivian's father, or it would give him more ammunition to be angry with her.

"Full house! Beat that, dealer," Roger said with a grunt and a "Woo!"

Michael congratulated him and placed his winnings in

front of him. My brother struggled with knowing when to quit. He grabbed the chips, his hands still a bit shaky as he stacked his winnings. The frustration seemed to melt into a quiet, almost stunned satisfaction.

I walked up behind him and whispered in his ear. "Now, quit while you're ahead."

He groaned and shook his head.

"I tried," I said to my mother who was standing behind me.

She nodded then whispered something in Roger's other ear and he got up and stepped away from the table. How did she do that? He was definitely a mama's boy. I knew he still had to be down a few hundred dollars. Gambling and alcohol did not mix when it came to my brother.

His demeanor quickly changed when just a few minutes later he had his arm around a cute blonde. At least he wasn't gambling. I walked around to check everything out before our band started again. Vivian's mother was calling out the winners of the raffle. Samantha won the trip for two to Hawaii. She made eyes at me, and I knew this was going to blow up in my face. She would ask me to go with her so I did what any avoider would do, I sat down in front of the microphone on the stage and began to talk to the crowd, thanking everyone for coming. The band followed my lead and made their way back to their spots on stage. Even Samantha.

Once our band started playing again, the dance floor filled and everyone seemed to be having a great time, even Roger. I watched Vivian's parents dancing away and it brought a smile to my face. How did she have any doubt whether or not the two of them were in love? It seemed obvious. Maybe they just avoided public displays of affection in front of their children.

In between sets, I helped out the kitchen and the servers. A lot of the workers were friends of Vivian's but not all of them had experience working at a restaurant. All in all, the turnout was great and we pulled it off. The red-carpet entrance into the restaurant was an even bigger hit with #Zenithbarandgrill trending all over social media.

Two in the morning, Vivian finally took a break in her office. I sat down on the chair across from her desk. This was the first break both of us had all night.

"This was the busiest I have ever seen the bar since it opened. The 007 theme was quite the hit," Vivian said with excitement.

"I heard from multiple people they felt like they were stepping right into a Bond movie when they walked in. The red carpet and professional pictures were a great touch. I've never seen a fundraiser like this before. You killed it."

She smiled. "This may be repetitious, but I couldn't have done it without you or my family."

"I would say you raised well over what we expected. The silent auction was a big success, too."

"I hope so. But even if this doesn't work out, I can honestly say I fought as hard as I could. I can't be disappointed in that."

"Absolutely. Congratulations."

"I won't be able to sleep after this," I said. "Want to come to my house for an after bar?"

She laughed. "I don't remember the last time I went to an after-bar party. My early twenties maybe."

"I'm having the band over, and I'm inviting everyone who worked tonight. It'll be fun. You should definitely come. Celebrate all the success today."

"Okay, you talked me into it. Now, let's count this money."

# CHAPTER 23

## *Vivian*

LIAM'S DRIVEWAY was full of cars. Most of my employees must have accepted his invitation. Music blared before I even opened up my car door. Colored lights flashed through the windows and cut into the dark night.

I could feel spring in the air and on my feet as I accidentally stepped in a puddle and soaked my foot. Why didn't I bring my flats? I'd been on my feet all night in heels, and I was ready to rip them off and throw them in the trash. I struggled to walk with a blister burning on the heel of my left foot. As soon as I walked in the door I kicked off my heels, helped myself to a seltzer, and collapsed on an open couch.

Fatigue threatened to overwhelm me. I'd been going strong for days while we organized for the event, and it showed tonight. I was so grateful for all the support I received. The fundraiser was the most successful event I'd ever put on. And we made close to fifty thousand dollars. I prayed it was enough for a down payment. It had to be.

Alyssa came and sat next to me. "What a night. It's more than what we hoped for. Good job."

"I didn't do it alone. I must say I was surprised at the turnout. I've never seen my restaurant so packed."

"I'm exhausted but that was unbelievable. Maybe you should start a party planning business instead."

I laughed. "No thanks. I'll just keep my restaurant."

Alyssa held up her glass. "To the Zenith Bar and Grill continuing to kick on for another decade."

"I hope so. To the bar," I said and clinked my can with her glass.

"Are you going to take a risk and celebrate for real tonight?" She nodded in Liam's direction.

My face warmed. "What is up with all you matchmakers? Liam and I are just friends."

"Mm-hmm," she said in disbelief.

"What? We are."

Liam walked over to us and Alyssa jumped off the couch and headed in the opposite direction.

Liam nodded at Alyssa's back. "What did I do?"

"Nothing. She's just being weird. Have a seat," I said, patting the couch next to me.

He sat down next to me and put his arm around the back of the couch behind me.

"You must be exhausted. All that work and now it's over. I have a feeling the bank is going o have no problem giving you that loan."

I let out a sigh. "Yeah, still seems too good to be true. I'll celebrate once I know for sure."

"I get it."

"I want to apologize for the other day."

He waved me off. "Don't worry about it. You know where I stand."

"Yeah. I—"

"Liam, everyone is begging for you to sing a couple songs. I put your guitar on the table," Samantha said, intentionally interrupting us. The woman obviously had a crush on him the way she giggled at everything he said all night. Like a teenager, she was always trying to put her hands on him.

"Oh, and I'm not sure if you noticed but I won the trip to Hawaii for two."

"Mm, hmm," he said, blowing her off. He looked at me and rolled his eyes, obviously annoyed she kept pushing.

I pushed him gently to help him get away. "You better get over there. Do your thing. They're waiting."

He looked back at me and smiled. His smile took my breath away and so did his singing. Samantha followed him like a puppy, turning back to flick her hair and give me a snooty look.

This time he sat in a chair in front of the fireplace, his guitar in his lap. The room went quiet.

"This song is for the woman in my life I can't stop thinking about. She's kind and beautiful, smart and everything I've ever wanted in a woman. May she one day see that I'll never break her heart, and I want to wake up with her by my side for the rest of my life." His eyes twinkled in the light as they met mine. "Take a chance on me, Vivian. This is my grand gesture and the last time I will ask. The ball is in your court now."

Everyone looked my way, and I froze in shock.

Samantha glared at me and shook her head.

He started playing, and my heart went into overdrive as an electric current shot through my body. He began playing *Thinking Out Loud* by Ed Sherran. I backed up until I ran into something and turned around to find Alyssa standing there.

Alyssa hit my arm. "I can't believe he had the balls to do that. I didn't think he had it in him."

Me neither. I wanted to run but running never worked for me. Tears ran down my cheek. I wiped them away. He was still staring right at me. I stood frozen, my body numb. My heart ached at his words, but my head told me to stop being a fool. As soon as he played the last note I got up and walked out of the living room and down the hall to the bathroom. I was unsure how to face him. What to say. I was more confused than ever before.

I shut the door and stared at myself in the mirror. I didn't deserve this. I didn't deserve him. I'd run and break his heart. The moment I walked in that door and found my ex in bed with someone else flashed in my head when I tried to imagine a happily ever after. Happy was not in my cards.

A knock on the door had me glancing in the mirror to make sure to wipe away any evidence that I had been crying.

"One second," I said, washing my hands.

I opened the door and there he stood staring at me with a look of concern in his eyes. "You okay?"

I nodded and pushed a smile.

"Let's go somewhere where we can talk."

He led me down the hall to the back door.

He led me outside to the gazebo. The fireplace was electric and the screen of wood on logs set the mood. The outdoor furniture was stored in here with a bar in the corner and a gray sectional. I sat down on the closest spot to the fireplace, and he sat down next to me, like he had this all planned out.

"I'm sorry if the song was too much. I wanted to give you one last confession. Now I'll back off, I—"

I'm not sure if it was the romantic vibe or the way he sang to me, but I could no longer hold back. I pulled him toward me by his collar and kissed him. He stiffened, then relaxed and wrapped his arms around me. The kiss stopped my brain from working and my mind from overthinking. Our mouths were made for each other.

I pushed him back on the couch and straddled him between my legs. I stared into his beautiful eyes, and he pushed my hair behind my shoulders. I leaned in and kissed him again. Just to remind myself of the taste of his mouth.

He took my face in his hands and he kissed up my neck until he reached my ear. He bit my earlobe gently. My body felt warm all over.

I once again pulled back so I could look into his eyes. Everything about this night felt like a dream. He reached behind me and unzipped my dress and pulled it over my head.

I should have stopped him but I wanted more. If we made love, would our friendship be over?

His kisses took me out of my own head, and I relaxed to his touch.

I pushed him back and ripped open his dress shirt. A couple buttons went flying and I ran my hands down his naked chest and slipped it over his shoulders until it fell behind him. I ran my hands all over his torso until I made it down to his belt. I traced the indents that disappeared beneath his pants.

He groaned with pleasure

My fingers ran down his arms, and he flexed for me. How long did I dream of squeezing these arms? My nails dug into his back as I kissed him even deeper. A grunt escaped from deep in his throat. I laughed.

"You like what you do to me, don't you, Viv? Well, this is what I'm going to do to you." He smothered me with a kiss and guided me to my back on the couch. He was laying on top of me. I wrapped my legs around him, and he lifted up my bra.

"You're so damn beautiful, you know that?"

"You're acting like you've never seen me naked before."

He chuckled. "Hey, I turned away. It's not my fault you took off all your clothes and jumped into the shower with me."

My body stiffened, and I pushed him away. "What? Are you serious?"

"Yes, that was challenging. I really had to dig deep for self-control."

"I took off all my clothes and jumped into the shower with

you, and you walked away?" How did I not remember this? "The night I got wasted and you stayed over?"

"Yeah, the night you puked all over me and then told me I smelled like vomit." He laughed again.

I covered my face. "I'm so embarrassed. This definitely ruined the moment."

"I'm sorry." He tucked the hair on my face behind my ear so gently it left me with goosebumps.

"Don't be. I'm not complaining."

He pulled me close and kissed me again. He devoured my mouth and steamed up the room.

I was out of breath when we finally stopped kissing. His hands began to explore my body. Waves of desire rolled over me.

We undressed and lay naked on the floor.

"Can I make love to you, Miss Vivian?"

No reply was needed. I showed him I was ready. Our bodies fit together perfectly, and our hearts were finally aligned.

I never in my life had sex like that, and I woke up the next morning covered in an Afghan with nothing but anxiety over the line we'd both crossed. I'd never see Liam the same way again. He changed me that night.

I slipped out of his arms and dressed before turning back for one last look at his strong jawline and naked chest. I shut the door, careful not to wake him, and walked away.

# CHAPTER 24

## *Liam*

I WAS NAKED AND ALONE. Had I had dreamed it all? I sat up to see if maybe she was nearby, but she was gone. I put on my clothes and went inside my house, but she was long gone as I expected. Ran away again for the second time. I was never going to learn my lesson.

I kept myself busy the next week with all the work I had to do. The end of April came way too quickly. Just five days remained until the deadline for taxes. I had taken some time off from the restaurant so I hadn't seen Vivian since that night. I texted to let her know I could work on Friday, and she responded with, Sounds good!! Two exclamations. Did that mean she was happy about it? Passive aggressive? I shook it off and got back to work. I would never understand women.

The bell rang and since I was the only one in the office, I had to stop in the middle of my work to greet another customer. If one more last-minute person came in begging to get their taxes completed before the deadline I was going to lose it.

I stopped mid-step as soon as I saw those brown curls bounce. "Viv? What are you doing here?"

"I wanted to apologize."

"Apologize, for what?"

She fidgeted and looked around the room. "Is this a good time? I know you're busy. I can come back," she said. "It was really rude of me to just show up. I don't know what I was thinking."

"You're fine, really. Is everything okay?" She was trying to run again.

"Yeah, but I needed to talk to you. I feel like such a jerk that I left without saying goodbye after…"

"After we slept together?"

Her face blushed a cute red. "Yeah. After that." She bit her lip and looked away as if she was worried about what I would say next. Was she afraid I wanted more now? She was not ready to commit to a relationship. That was written all over her face.

"Don't look so scared. I know what happened doesn't change anything, and I want you to know I'm not going to keep pushing you. I know you just want to be friends."

A big fat lie, but I wanted her to tell me I was wrong. That she wanted to be with me. She was emotionally unavailable and permanently running from love, literally.

"You're right. We made a mistake. I never should have—"

"Slept with me?" I shrugged to let her know it was fine even though it was not fine.

"Um…well…you know me. I'm not exactly dating material," she murmured.

It took everything in me to bite my tongue and let her talk until I could walk away. I needed to walk away this time before she did again. Fire burned in my chest. "Listen, can we talk for a second?"

She raised an eyebrow. "Everything okay?"

"Yeah. I just—"

Her phone rang in her pocket. "Give me one quick minute, okay?"

Would I ever come first?

She stepped out into the hallway and shut the door. I waited five minutes, but no Vivian. I peeked my head out the door to see her standing outside the door with her back against the wall.

"Is everything okay?"

She blinked back tears. "Yeah, fine. It's nothing. Now, you wanted to talk to me about something?"

We stepped back into my office and I shut the door. "No, it can wait. Are you sure that was nothing? You don't look okay." I was worried about her. Something did not feel right. She was hiding something.

Her eyes flashed to anger. "Liam, everything is fine." She looked away and her expression softened as she inhaled deeply and slowly let it out before speaking. "I'm sorry. Please, tell me what it is you want to say. I'm all ears."

I shifted my weight from one foot to the other and looked down as I searched for the right words. "I'm putting in my two weeks as of this weekend."

Her mouth dropped. "What? Why? Is this because of me? Because we slept together? I just need time to process this, Liam. I don't want to ruin our friendship. See, this is exactly why I knew it would never work between the two of us."

"It's not that, Viv." I put my hand on her shoulder. "My business is falling apart. I had to file extensions on far too many clients' tax forms. If I stay, I'll end up losing my business and Roger will go down with me. He may be a jerk at times, but I can't let him down. We've both worked too hard."

She bit her lip, her eyes saddened as if she felt at fault.

"Viv, it's not your fault. It's not you."

She nodded, her eyes were clearly filling with tears she was trying so hard to blink away.

She took my hand and squeezed it. "I get it, Liam. You need to do what's best for you. I'm going to miss you. I hope you know that. You're irreplaceable. But I'll be okay, the bar will be okay."

I looked into her eyes. If only I could take the pain away. Let her see this was what was best for not only me but her, too. My feelings were getting too big to just go back to being friends. She was right, us sleeping together was something we could not come back from. I wanted to be with her, and the regret of sleeping with me reflected on her face. But I did not want her to feel bad. It was not her fault she didn't think of me that way. A part of me hoped this changed things for us and she would give us a try, but I was kidding myself. I knew better and I needed my distance before she broke my heart again.

"Just promise me one thing," she said.

"What is that?"

"You'll still be my friend."

Her request stabbed me with a knife right through my heart. The word friend killed me and was why I needed to keep my distance. But I could never tell her why I had to leave.

"You will always be my friend. I just need a little space for a bit. You understand, right?" In other words, I needed some time to get over her or at least try.

This heartbreak left me in pain. My body physically hurt. No woman had ever made me feel this way before. If we hadn't slept together maybe we would have been okay. We could have taken it slower, but I was stupid and impulsive. I did not think it through. But did I regret the most wonderful night of my life? Would I do the same if I were to do it all over again? Yeah, I would because one night with her was better than never knowing what it felt like to make love to the woman I was madly in love with. I risked my heart for her, but she was not ready and she probably never would be.

She looked broken but forced a smile. "I'll do whatever you need. I should really get going."

She turned around and left, taking my heart with her as the door clicked behind her.

I stared out the window. The next two weeks would be long and torturous.

# CHAPTER 25
## *Vivian*

I PUSHED the down button on the elevator at least ten times before I gave up and booked it toward the stairs. But I went the wrong way at first. The elevator dinged behind me, and the tears burst from my eyes.

I had screwed up big time. I never should have slept with him. I knew how much he liked me, and it broke him. Didn't he see I wasn't worth loving? He was too good for me. I was not the person he thought I was.

I made it down the stairs in record time, trying to get away as fast as I could before anyone saw me. On the drive to the bar all I could think about was trying to run the bar without him. I cried with frustration. People were probably wondering what was going on as I drove by them in my car. Alyssa was great, but no one could replace Liam.

My phone rang through my car speaker. Tim. I pushed the button on my screen.

"Hey Tim," I said, fighting the tears that were still pooling in my eyes. I blinked away the blurriness in my vision and sniffed to clear my stuffy nose.

Tim laughed and shouted into the phone. "I've got news!"

"You do? Tell me," I said, doing my best to force excitement into my voice though I was not ready to hear anything exciting.

"Lizzy and I have finally set a date for our wedding."

I forced a smile as I said probably too enthusiastically, "Congratulations! It's about time. When are you getting married? Where?"

"This summer in Side Lake. We're thinking the fourth of July weekend. I know it

s soon, but when you know you know. We want an outdoor wedding."

"That's awesome, Tim. I'm so happy for you." I really was happy but it was hard to feel it in the moment.

"Is everything okay?'

A sob escaped and I started bawling.

"Viv, what's going on? Are you okay?"

I sobbed a few more times before I could get my voice to work. "I'm fine, just a little breakdown."

"I know something is bothering you. Don't hide it from me. Please talk to me."

"The bank called me today. It's—" I struggled to hold in another sob, but it escaped again. I could not say the words out loud.

"What happened? Didn't you make enough for a down-payment."

"I did, but someone offered them more. I couldn't match it, and I had to pass."

"What? You have to be kidding me. Won't the person buying it let you keep your restaurant?"

I shook my head. "I'm not sure. The bank didn't know. There's a small chance, so I need to figure out what I'm going to do with all this money I raised. If I shut down people will think I planned this. I don't know what to do. It was all for nothing."

"Don't overthink it. Did you tell Liam? He's an accoun-tant, right? He can help you figure this out. Maybe you could find another restaurant or this person who bought it will let you stay. Don't give up until you know for sure."

"Well, it's complicated with Liam. He doesn't work for me anymore."

"What?"

"He, uh, well…he put in his two weeks."

Tim cleared his throat. "What happened?"

"It's a long story but I messed up."

He paused for so long I thought the phone had cut out. His voice came out more of a whisper. "You need to fix this, Vivian. You have to apologize for whatever you did. He's a good one. If not, let me know and I'll come down there myself and try to figure this out."

I did not want him to come and put his nose into my business. This was my problem, and I needed to figure it out. "No, you're right. I'll fix this. I promise. Thank you for your help. I needed it. I'll talk to Liam."

"Are you sure?"

"Yes." My voice cracked. "And Tim, I can't wait for your wedding. It's going to be perfect.

I really was happy for him, but at the moment his happiness made me feel so small. Would I ever have what he had? Did I even want that? I liked my independence but sometimes I felt lonely. Even thinking about having to date again and play the dating game made me sick to my stomach. I made sure to date men who would not get attached because I wanted to have fun and live in the now. Still Jimmy hurt me, so I wasn't ready to get back into the dating pool. Even if it was just to swipe left, maybe right occasionally on Tinder or some other dating app.

I knew I should talk to Liam like I promised, but I needed more time. I might be losing my bar, and I was pretty sure there was nothing Liam or anyone else could do. I had already asked him to do so much, but it wasn't his job to save me twice.

"And Viv, one more thing. Hang on."

"Will you be one of my bridesmaids?" Lizzy said, her voice sweet. "Before you answer, I want you to know I want all your sisters in the wedding. I know that isn't a great situation because of your feuding, but I want you to know upfront before you make this decision."

"I can't' speak for my sisters, but I'll be there. I'm honored. Just don't be hurt if any of them say no. It's been rough between us. Family feuds are the worst."


Liam was busy leaning over the bar, serving a group of beautiful women sitting on the bar stools. One was leaning forward, her chest resting right on the bar, so her cleavage was in full display for Liam. I'm sure he was grinning ear to ear, but I tried my best not to pay any attention. To look away. Even if it was all I could think about.

I stocked the coolers while he continued to chat and serve drinks.

I jumped when he threw the bar rag next to the sink. "I'll be right back, I'm going to get these ladies another case of Bent Paddle."

"Blame it on me. I love my beer," the blonde said.

He smiled back at them before disappearing around the corner. I went back to stocking the last case.

"I can't wait to see his muscles rip when he carries that beer back. Damn he's hot," one of the women said.

"You should give him your number. He's gorgeous. Unless you think he's taken," the other one said.

"Excuse me, Miss? Miss?"

Were they talking to me?

I turned around to find they were indeed speaking to me. And here I thought I was invisible. I walked over to them. "Need something?"

The blonde giggled. "Yeah, is Liam single?"

I couldn't help myself. "No."

Yep, I said it. There was no taking it back now. Why would I say that? He was not in a relationship, but they needed to back off. I was protecting him. They could have a husband or a STD. They could be psychologically insane for all I knew. I was doing him a favor, and I was in no way jealous.

The brunette pouted. "He's not single? I didn't see a ring though."

The blonde chewed on her lip, deep in thought. "I mean, if he's not wearing a ring it must not be very serious, right?"

She was not addressing anyone in particular with her words. She seemed to be justifying what was yet to come. I had to put a stop to this.

"He's my boyfriend," I said through clenched teeth and a look that would make most people run in the opposite direction. "Hands off or else," I said in my most threatening tone.

I turned around and bumped right into Liam who had a case of beer hanging from each hand.

"Hi, Honey," he said, a smirk on his face.

Oh crap. I was totally busted. He heard me. How was I going to explain myself to him? I don't even know why I said that. I wished I could take it back but the thought of those bimbos having their hands all over him or passing him their phone number made my chest burn. What was wrong with me?

I shook my head at him as heat burned on my neck and face.

"I see you ladies met my fiancé," he said, his eyes still on me.

Fiancé? He was going to play this game. Wasn't he?

"I was sure you were single," the blonde said.

The brunette produced another exaggerated pout. "All the hot ones are taken or gay. Have fun with him." She turned to Liam and winked, not even hiding it from me, the fiancé.

"Well, if you ever happen to break up give me a call, handsome." She held out a piece of paper and shoved it into the front pocket of his khaki pants.

I looked at his face, unable to see her hand from my angle. He grunted and backed away.

I'm pretty sure she squeezed a lot more than just a pocket. I wanted to walk right over there and put her in her place. But somehow, I dug deep for self-control.

# CHAPTER 26

## *Liam*

I WENT into the kitchen and put my hands on the wall waiting for the pain to ease. She literally squeezed everything, and the shooting pain was getting more intense.

I heard a laugh behind me and there stood Vivian with her arms crossed and a giant grin on her face.

I couldn't help myself. "You're boyfriend, huh?"

"Shush. I was saving you from those hot women." Her face reddened.

The pain was suddenly tolerable. I even let a smirk slip.

"Yeah, wouldn't want to be subjected to beautiful women." I took a step closer to her and flicked a small piece of fuzz off her shoulder.

The ball was still in her court.

"I should probably work on some administrative stuff," she said, pointing behind her. "Let me know if it gets busy and you need my help."

Nothing had changed. I thought from her whole boyfriend comment she had changed her mind about me, but I should have known better. She was never going to change.

. . .

At around eleven, Jimmy came into the bar and sat in front of me on a bar stool. I puffed my chest out and inched my way closer to him. "You aren't welcome here."

He grinned up at me and started laughing.

"What's so funny?"

He turned his head to the side, his arms crossed. "Ready, Viv?"

My eyebrows drew down and inward. "What? Vivian, tell me you aren't going somewhere with this creep."

Her eyes flicked away from mine and dropped to the floor.

I did a double-take. "Are you kidding me? He attacked you, remember?"

A guilty look spread across her face. "Can I speak with you for a quick second, Liam?"

I followed her around the corner, but I kept an eye on Jimmy. She sure as hell was not going with him.

She hung her head. "Listen, I'll be fine. Trust me, okay? I know what I'm doing. I don't have time to explain."

I shook my head at her. "It's not that I don't trust you or think you can't handle yourself. He assaulted you, and it could have been really bad if I hadn't been there. I can't let you go with him."

"Liam, I'm not your woman, and you aren't the boss of me. I'm a big girl, and I can take care of myself. I know what I'm doing."

She stomped away from me and back to the bar without even caring what I had to say.

"Ready?"

I watched them walk out the door, and my fists clenched at my sides. I locked up and made my way to my car.

What was going on with her? Why was she trusting Jimmy after what he did? I rested my head on my hand as I leaned against my car window and stared out into the darkness. There had to be a reason why she was with him. I knew her better than that. Either he was blackmailing her, manipulating her, or she needed something from him. Unless she just needed his forgiveness? No, I highly doubted that.

She was gone and there was nothing I could do. If something happened. I'd never forgive myself for letting her go without a bigger fight. I picked up my phone.

"Hello?"

"Hey Tim, it's Liam."

"Liam, hey. I'm so glad Viv came around to talking to you. I thought she'd be too stubborn. Do you think you can help her then?"

What in the world was he talking about? "Help her?"

He laughed. "You know, with the financials."

"Huh?" I was so confused.

"For the restaurant. You know, since someone put in a higher bid than what she could afford."

"Oh, that." Someone was buying the building from under her? Who would do that? I was so confused. She never said a word to me about it. When did this happen?

"Yeah. Do you think there's anything you can do to get the building if they haven't signed anything yet? Last I heard it still sounded like an agreement wasn't finalized yet. Hopefully it isn't too late."

There was still a chance. Did this have something to do with Jimmy? No. He didn't have enough money or credit to buy the place. Did he?

"Do you know that Jimmy guy Vivian was dating?"

The line went quiet. Tim finally whispered, "Yeah. Why? Don't tell me they're back together again."

"Actually, the opposite. He came into the restaurant the other night and tried to attack Vivian, so I kicked him out."

"That bastard."

"But today he came to the bar looking for her, and she willingly went with him with a smile on her face."

Tim groaned. "I swear I'm going to kill that guy. I'm going to hang up and call her now."

"No, don't," I said. "I already tried that, but it won't help. She likely won't answer. What I'm trying to say is I think Jimmy has something to do with all of this. Could he get his hands on a lot of money? Does he have a lot of money that you know of?"

Tim let out a deep exhale. "I'm pretty sure he's a drug dealer so my guess is yes. And I wouldn't put it past him to do whatever he could to get Vivian back. He's probably black-mailing her."

I hit the steering wheel in reaction to his words, hurting my hand. I groaned in pain. "I knew it. Listen, you call Vivian, but don't tell her you know anything. I have an idea."

"Liam, what are you going to do? This is my sister you're talking about. I should be there."

I looked around to make sure no one could hear me. "No. Do you trust me?"

"Liam, I hardly know you."

"But do you trust that I care about Viv?"

The phone went quiet and then he whispered, "Yes. For some reason I do."

"Then let me handle the restaurant. I won't let Jimmy get the restaurant, okay? But please don't say anything to her. Promise?"

"Fine, but you aren't going to do anything illegal, are you?"

I laughed. "I don't plan on it, but I'd do anything for her. There are no limits when it comes to your sister."

"I had a feeling you'd say that. She never talked to you about the buyer. Did she?"

How could she not tell me? "No. I figured it out."

"Okay. I trust you. You must really love my sister, or you're a saint."

I smiled. "You can thank me when she never has to talk to that psycho again. Now, make sure she's okay."

"Deal. And Liam?"

"Yeah."

"Take care of my sister. Watch out for her."

My silence was enough to let him know that was exactly my plan. I hung up and drove to Vivian's apartment and spent the rest of the night in my car watching her come home and go up to her apartment. I saw Olivia in the window with Melody twice, rocking her to sleep. I would have to tell her they needed to draw their curtains at night. What if Jimmy had been watching them?

Vivian came home alone, Jimmy nowhere in sight. At least she was smart in that regard. Once the sun came up, I made my way to the bank. Time to drain my savings. I'd worked hard to build up my bank account, but it was just money. Vivian needed my help. Even if it cost me my own business in the process.

# CHAPTER 27
## *Vivian*

I **FELT** horrible for lying to Liam. I left him with disbelief and worry in his eyes, but I had no choice. I promised Jimmy I would not tell anyone or the deal was off. Liam would understand eventually. All night I kept looking at my phone to see if he was texting me.

Jimmy and I sat down at a table in the corner of Bent Paddle on the west side of Duluth. I loved beer that was brewed locally, and I loved supporting my community. I cringed sitting across the table from the creep. The way he stared into my eyes made my skin crawl. This was once a guy I chose for myself.

My issues with romantic relationships were staring me right in the face, literally.

I put it out there the minute we sat down and ordered a beer. "I don't plan on staying long. What is it you want, Jimmy?"

He smiled, knowing he was in full control.

"I want another chance. I want full control of the bar, and I want you to turn it into a biker bar."

"Absolutely not."

He snorted. "It's so cute you think you have a choice."

What a jerk. "Is there no room for negotiation? Is this your final offer?"

He leaned back in his chair. "That's my final offer."

I stood up and placed a ten-dollar bill on the table. "I would rather lose my bar than partner up with you. I came here today to find out your offer so I'd have no regrets in the future when I turned you down and closed my bar. Thank you for that. A biker bar? Really? I own a family sports bar, Jimmy. A biker bar isn't even close to what my customers want. I won't sell my soul to the devil."

He did not move, but his smile widened. Why was he so cocky?

"Sit down, Vivian."

I leaned forward, my hands resting on the table. I clenched my teeth together. "I will not sit down. If those are your conditions, I'm out of here. I pushed past my chair and took two steps before he called out my name, but there was no turning back.

I put on my blinker and looked in my side mirror before I pulled out. There he was, running after me. I turned onto the road. No regrets. I would never negotiate with him. Not ever. Funny how he never had any money when we were together, but now he could buy my whole building and put me out of business just to spite me. I knew it had to be drug money, which I would not be a part of.

Pain and numbness over having to give up everything I stood for washed over me. All the blood, sweat, and tears I had put into my restaurant, the friends I'd gained along the way from employees and customers would be gone. I felt like I let everyone down and I had no idea what I was going to do with the money from the fundraiser. Maybe someday I could open up a restaurant in a new location, but I did not have it in me to do that right now. It took a lot to put together my business, and it took years to build up my clientele for the location. No matter what, I would never go low enough to sleep with the devil…again anyway.

I shut myself in my office and started writing a speech for my staff. Breaking the news to them again would hurt. Not only were they losing their jobs but their work family. We all got along so well. Most of my staff had families to support. This was the hard part about being the boss. I had the responsibility of breaking their hearts and delivering the devastating news. My eyes watered as I typed up the letter.

My phone vibrated on the table three times before I finally took a look at the screen. Tim. Twelve missed texts from him and three phone calls. I grabbed my phone off the table and put it up to my ear.

"Everything okay?"

His voice was shaky as he said, "Vivian, it's about time you picked up your phone. I've been worried about you! I'm on my way to Duluth right now."

"Why? What do you mean?"

"I heard about Jimmy."

"What?" Damn it, Liam. "It isn't what you think."

"Did you really take off with Jimmy after he attacked you?"

Okay, maybe it was exactly what he thought. "Yes, but I had a good reason."

I heard a knock on my office door.

"Hang on one second. Someone is at my door. I opened it to find Tim standing there with his arms crossed.

"May I come in?"

I stepped back and shut the door behind him.

He paced my office, his foot tapping impatiently and his eyebrows raised. "Well?"

"Listen, you didn't need to come all the way here. Jimmy put in an offer on the building that I couldn't compete against. I had to hear what he had to offer, but I knew it would never be an offer that would be to my benefit. I was right and I turned him down. That was all it was."

He gritted his teeth and anger flashed in his eyes. "After he attacked you? You went with him all by yourself? You know better than that. What if he had done something to you?"

I crossed my arms. Now I was getting angry. "But he didn't."

Tim ran his fingers through his hair. "But he could have. Why didn't you call me first? Damn it, Viv. Promise me you didn't do anything stupid."

"I didn't. I already told you that. I'm not dumb enough to get into bed with the devil." Okay, maybe that was a bad choice of words.

His jaw tightened and a muscle flickered in his cheek as he stared at me. His eyes were hard, and he stopped blinking.

"Okay, not exactly the best choice of words, but I told him no. I'm not going to be controlled by him. It's non-negotiable."

"Good. What about the restaurant?"

"I'm done. Maybe one day I'll open up another one, but I'm exhausted. Maybe I'll get a job that has less pressure. Work for someone else for a while. I live and breathe this place. From the moment I wake up until I go to bed all I can think about is this place. I can't start from scratch right now. I'm okay with it."

He eyed me curiously, trying to read me. "Are you?"

"I mean, I wouldn't choose to close down my restaurant and I fought hard to save it, but I can't give in to Jimmy. I won't."

"I agree."

I'm not sure exactly what I expected him to say but it wasn't that. That was too easy.

"Listen, let's head down to the bank together and find out if there's anything we can do. Give it one last try."

I nodded. "Just let me grab a jacket."

Tim opened my car door for me, and I crawled in. "They're predicting the snowstorm this weekend will be a big downfall. Close to two feet."

I watched him walk around to the driver's side door and get in.

"They always say that."

"In April? We don't get snow in April."

"Are you kidding me, Tim? Where have you been all these years? There's always one last snowstorm in April."

We walked into the bank and waited a few minutes until a customer service agent greeted us. "Vivian? Nice to see you again." He reached out and shook my hand.

"This is my brother, Tim."

"Welcome, Tim. Please follow me."

We sat down at his desk while he typed into his computer. "About the building that houses your restaurant, it looks here like a second party overbid the original bid by a significant amount of money."

My eyes bulged in my head. "What? Why does everyone want my building so much? Are there diamonds in the wall or something?"

Tim laughed under his breath.

"How much did they overbid?"

The banker wrote down the dollar amount and showed us.

I leaned over to Tim and whispered, "I can't top that."

He nodded in agreement. "Does this buyer want her to stay and run her restaurant, or do they have other ideas for the place?"

The banker stood. "Let me see what I can find out. Just give me a quick minute.

Close to five minutes later he finally returned. "Sorry

about that. Looks like the new owner wants you to stay. He's willing to sign a Business Purchase Agreement."

"What is that exactly?"

"He's pretty much selling it to you for a very reasonable price, less than what he bought it for. The buyer must be someone who loves your restaurant."

Who would have done something so selfless like this for a stranger?

Once we left the bank, I turned to Tim. "Don't you think this is a little weird that someone would do this out of the kindness of their heart?"

"Yes."

"Then why do you think they did this? What do they have to gain?"

His smile widened. My brother was handsome like my father, and seeing him smiling again was great, but the anticipation was killing me.

"Well?"

"I have a feeling you'll find out soon."

"What do you mean? Tim, do you know something you aren't telling me?"

# CHAPTER 28

## Liam

I **KNEW** she was going to kill me for doing this behind her back. But at least Tim would have my back when she found out. What did I just do? My phone dinged.

*Tim: YOU BOUGHT HER BUILDING???*

*Liam: I don't know what you're talking about….*

*Tim: SURE! I love you, man! Vivian is freaking out right now. You may want to tell her soon. She has no idea who bought the building, but she's suspicious.*

*Liam: I'm not telling her anything, and you better not either.*

*Tim: You have my word. but you better do something soon.*

*Liam: I will. I promise. Thanks. So she's happy, huh?*

*Tim: And confused.*

Vivian was freaking out and when I told her, she would want to kill me. But what else could I do? Let Jimmy take her bar with drug money? Not happening. She lived her life for the bar. I did what I had to so the bar and restaurant remained hers.

Unless Tim opened his big fat mouth, she would have no clue I was the secret buyer. If she found out, she would fight me on it and in no way was I letting that happen.

I started a short shift at noon on Sunday. Business was notoriously slow on Sundays, but I was hoping Vivian would be too busy to tell me about someone buying her building. About how she would be able to make payments and eventually own the place. I hated lying to her but I also did not want her to find out and turn my offer down.

Vivian did not arrive at the bar until three o'clock, just when I starting to think she was still avoiding me. She waved hello but headed for her office and shut the door.

Alyssa made her way behind the bar with fresh cut lemons and limes to replenish the fruit trays for topping off the drinks. "Did Viv talk to you yet?"

I struggled to breathe. "No, why?"

She did a double take. "Why are you acting weird? She has some good news."

I shot her a confused look.

"Fine, but don't tell her I told you. I'm sure she wants to be the one to break the news, but I'm ecstatic and I'm tickled she told me before you."

I shook my head at her. "Spit it out."

She looked around and then leaned close to my ear. "Someone bought the building and is letting Vivian make payments so she can own it. Isn't that so—"

She stopped and stared at me. I could feel my face growing hot the longer she stared at me. I wrinkled up my face, doing my best to keep a straight face but the guilt was eating me alive. "What? Why are you staring at me?"

Her lips shifted upward into a smile that widened until she shook her head and laughed at me. She plopped lemons into the dish. "How did I not catch this before. You're sly, Liam. You know that?"

I struggled to hide my smirk. Busted. "I'm not sure what you're talking about."

She studied me. "You aren't planning on telling her, are you?"

"Tell who what? What are you insinuating, Alyssa?"

She picked up the empty bowl. "Okay, I'll play your game. But be careful. If you don't tell her what you did, she may end up hating you." She leaned in close to my face. "I didn't know you had it in you. What did you do? Empty out your savings?"

I did not respond, no need to. She knew.

"You really are head over heels for her, aren't you?"

She disappeared around the counter, not waiting for an answer and knowing she would never get one from me.

Was it really that obvious? If it was that easy for Alyssa to figure out, how long would it take Vivian?

At the same time Vivian came around the bar, Samantha sat down in front of me. "Mimosa, please."

I opened up a new bottle of champagne, poured it in a flute and topped it off with orange juice and a slice of orange.

She grasped the flute and put the orange in her mouth. "You know an orange slice doesn't actually go on the rim of a mimosa, right?"

"Actually, it's the perfect garnish for a mimosa and enhances the presentation. Some bartenders even dip the rim in orange juice and sugar."

"Hmm. If I didn't know better, I'd think you actually like being a bartender."

I raised my eyebrows. "I do."

Samantha was my high school sweetheart, and we dated a couple years into college, but we broke up because we were both so young. After my parents passed and I went into a deep depression and quit the band, she did everything she could to be there for me, but I was broken. Unable to love. And that was not fair to her so I broke it off. She would always be one of my best friends, but the romantic connection was gone.

"What brings you in today to criticize my bartending skills?"

"I miss you, Liam."

I smiled and put my hand on top of hers. "I miss you, too. Having the band back together was great. Thank you for doing that."

She gave me a sad smile. "I'd do anything for you, Liam. You know that."

"Same."

She cleared her throat and gulped down her mimosa. "Another, please."

As I made another drink, she stared at me with sad eyes. "What you said after the fundraiser at your house, when you sang with your guitar."

I froze for a moment, trying to remember, my eyes fixed on her with a blank stare. I shook my head, hoping she would describe whatever it is she was talking about because I was clueless.

She looked at her glass and rubbed her thumb over the perspiration on the outside. Her nervousness was hard to miss.

"The confession you made about the bar owner."

"Oh, Vivian."

Her lips formed into a straight line. "Yeah, her. Are you guys together?"

Why was she being so weird? Sure, I'd had my heart broken many times in my life, but Samatha was not around enough to be this concerned about my love life.

"No."

"I see. Are you hung up on her?" Her eyes were now staring deep into mine.

"Vivian and I would never work. She's made that clear."

"Well, she's stupid. Any girl who would turn you down during a romantic gesture like that is an idiot."

She downed the rest of her drink then put a twenty-dollar bill on the bar. "You're one of a kind, Liam. I haven't stopped thinking about you since we broke up. I don't want you to answer now but I want to give us another try."

"I—"

She leaned over the bar and put her finger against my lips. "Shush. Please, don't say anything back, okay? I want you to take your time and think about us. If you want to go out to dinner sometime just give me a call, okay?"

I nodded, not sure what to say. Sure, she was flirting with me the night of the fundraiser but Samantha was always flirting with me. Her attention was flattering, but I never thought of anything beyond that. I had my eyes set on someone else. Someone who did not want me back. I was so dumb. Samantha was a good friend. She was beautiful and kind and sweet, and she was there for me after my parents died. I pushed her away, but here she was, still waiting for me.

"Okay," I said, still in shock. I never expected such a confession from her. Nor did I have any idea how to reply. I knew how bad it hurt to tell someone how much you like them only to get rejected. I could not do that to her right now.

What was I going to say? I knew what it was like to be on the other side of this.

She looked over her shoulder and saw Vivian coming in. Instead of leaving, she giggled and said, "What are your plans for the night? I'd like to hang out."

Here we go.

# CHAPTER 29

## *Vivian*

I WALKED into the bar area only to find him talking to his ex-girlfriend. The pain in my chest hit hard. It took everything in me to back up and disappear around the corner. He'd moved on, and the way she was making eyes at him told me everything I needed to know. It made sense. I turned him down and he was done waiting for me. Did I blame him? I was making the right decision. I'd come back later when she was gone to tell him the good news, even if he only had one week left working at the bar. The thought made me weak.

It was better this way. The torture of seeing him every day would no longer be an issue when I knew it would never last between us.

Samantha was beautiful, a brunette with a whole lot of curves that most women only dreamed of or resorted to plastic surgery to get. Her demeanor toward me turned cold after Liam announced his feelings for me the night of the fundraiser. She wanted him back. He never told me why they broke up and although I was curious, not knowing was better. Plus, it was years ago.

Why did I keep thinking about him?

She glanced my way and gave me the side eye when I returned. I had no choice but to acknowledge her presence. Let her know I was okay with her and that I was not her competition. "Samantha, right?" I said with a forced smile.

"Hi. Veronica, is it?"

I cleared my throat. She wanted to play this game. I could play this game. "Vivian, actually."

"Hmm. I was just telling Liam I'm sure you wouldn't mind if he got off early so he could take me out to dinner. Isn't that right, Liam?"

He avoided eye contact with me and refused to reply.

Samantha raised her eyebrows at me, challenging me. "Well?"

I looked to Liam, but he still gave me no indication of whether or not he wanted to go with her. He was a big boy and I would not be the jealous one. "I can cover if you want to go early, Liam. Alyssa and I can handle it."

His eyes finally focused on mine and disappointment showed on his face.

Why would that upset him? It made no sense. He hardly even looked my way to give me any idea whether or not he wanted to go early. I held my breath, hoping he would stay, but his cold stare burned right through my heart and left me with chills.

"Let me get my jacket," he said.

He walked past me, purposely avoiding any interaction with me. This was the first time I ever saw him so cold. He hated me.

I followed him into the break room. No way was I letting him leave like this. Couldn't he see he was breaking me?

His back was toward me as he pulled his jacket off the hook

"Liam, can we talk?"

He stilled, but he did not turn around.

"Liam?" I said louder.

He finally turned and looked at me.

"Did I do something wrong? If you didn't want to go you should have told me. I don't want you to leave, but I also don't want to stop you."

He shook his head at me, and his scrunched up smile turned into a thin line. "Everything is fine."

He was so cold.

"Now, if you will excuse me."

I turned to the side to let him slip past me.

"Liam," I said and he turned around. My heart was beating right out of my chest. I could feel it pulsating in my head.

He started turning away when I just stood there like an idiot. "Please don't go."

He turned back around and looked at me, a hint of curiosity in his expression. "Why?"

"You are my best friend, and this is killing me. Please talk to me."

"Vivian, I can't do this right now. I need some time, okay? Can't you see my heart is broken?"

His angry eyes turned vulnerable, sad. I covered my face with my hands and started crying. He rushed over and put his arms around me.

He put his forehead against mine. "I'm being an asshole right now, but it isn't your fault. You don't feel the same way about me that I feel about you. You can't help the way you feel."

I pulled my head away and wiped my eyes with the back of my hand. "But I don't want to lose you. You're my best friend."

I looked into his eyes, and he smiled back at me. A genuine smile. He pushed a curl behind my ear.

"You don't have any idea how beautiful you are. Do you?"

I smiled through my overflowing tears and blinked to see him through my cloudy vision. "How do I fix this?"

He rested his hand on my jawline and pulled my head up to look at him. "It's not a you- problem, Viv. It's me. I need some time to be broken, okay? Please, let me go. You'll always be my person, but I fell hard, and I need some space. Please, let me be upset for a little bit, okay?"

I nodded and told my feet to take a step back, but they had a mind of their own. I leaned forward and rested my lips on his. My arms wrapped around his neck, and I pulled him in to me softly. His arms wrapped around my back, and he picked me up. I reacted by wrapping my legs around his hips. He pushed me up against the back wall and kissed me harder. My body ached for him.

My hands started pulling his shirt out of his pants, but it was stuck. As the need overpowered me, I leaned back and ripped his shirt open, buttons popping once again. The need for his body on mine radiated through my veins. I had to have him right here and now.

His teeth bit into my lip with need, and the desire exploded inside me.

"Liam, the hot lady from the bar—"

We both turned our heads to see Alyssa standing at the doorway. Her jaw dropped and her eyes widened. "Why hello. It's about time."

Liam set me down and pulled on his shirt but half the buttons were gone.

Alyssa leaned into her hand to silence a laugh. "I think you missed a button or two there, Liam."

He looked up and glared at her.

"I'll let Samantha know you'll be a couple minutes," she said with a wink.

"No, tell her he's on his way." I straightened my shirt and tucked it into my pants.

Liam looked at me and frowned. He picked up his jacket and zipped it up over his half-buttoned shirt.

I wanted to say something, but I was unsure what to even say. My mind drew a blank. I threw my hand out to grab his arm, but he stepped away and toward the door.

At the door he turned and looked at me. "Bye, Vivian."

This time I did not try to stop him.

# CHAPTER 30

## *Liam*

I HAD A HEAVY JACKET ON, and I was a puddle of sweat. We were at Old Chicago in Canal Park, and I was unable to take off my jacket because I knew Samantha would have so many question as to why I was missing buttons on my shirt. Not that I cared what she thought, but I wasn't sure how I would even explain this to her. The image of Vivian pushed up against the wall, our hands all over each other, played over and over in my head.

A mistake, a moment of impulsive behavior for both of us. But damn her body felt so good. Her lips were so warm. "

What are you thinking about?"

Samantha's words interrupted my thoughts and brought me back to the present. "Nothing."

"Take off your jacket, stay a while," she said with flirty eyes.

"I'm cold."

My phone vibrating in my jacket pocket was a nice distraction. I pulled it out and looked at it. "Give me one second. I need to take this. Why don't you order a pizza for us and a Bent Paddle on tap for me.

She nodded and I stepped away, putting the phone up to my face. "Hello."

"Liam. What the hell? Did you tell Viv about the bar? She is freaking out, man, and I don't know what to tell her."

"Don't tell her anything, Tim," I said. "You don't need to tell her yet. You promised, man."

"I can't keep lying to my sister. She should know."

I was frustrated. "It's not your place, Tim. Listen, let me tell her when the time is right, okay? If she finds out it's me right now, she will be furious."

"Okay, fine," he whispered. "What's going on between the two of you? She said something about having a fallout."

"She said that?"

"Yeah. I don't know what's going on with you two, but I hope you have a plan. You need to tell her because if she finds out I knew and didn't tell her, you know my sister."

I did. I do. I thought I did.

"Calm down. She won't find out. Not yet. I'll tell her, I promise. You can blame me, but right now if I tell her she'll tell me not to buy the building, and Jimmy will end up with it."

He sighed into the phone. "Fine. I'll let you handle it. Just promise me you'll do what's best for her, okay?"

"I will," I said and hung up. I made my way back to Samantha. "Sorry about that."

Concern flashed in her eyes. "Who was that?"

"Viv's brother."

Her eyebrows raised. "Viv as in your boss, Viv?"

I took a sip of my beer and nodded.

She shook her head at me. "How do you even know him, and why is he calling you?"

Jealousy rippled through her voice.

"He's a friend."

I had no reason to tell her even though I trusted her. She seemed jealous and was acting like we were back in high school when we were dating. But I owed her no explanation. She was not my girlfriend.

She pursed her lips together. "Do you still have feelings for Vivian?"

Not what I was expecting her to say at all. Her words threw me off. "What?" I had heard her, but her words shocked me. "What does that have to do with anything?"

She looked down and made circles on the table with her fingernail. "I thought when you called to get the band back together you wanted to give us a second chance, too. Roger said—"

"Roger? What does Roger have to do with anything?"

"He told me at the fundraiser you still had feelings for me, but you were too scared to reach out, so you were getting the band back together as a grand gesture. He told me not to tell you."

That bastard.

"And then you sang that song for Vivian at the after party. I was heartbroken and confused."

I looked into her sad eyes. I really cared for this woman a long time ago.

"What you and I had was unbelievable and special. You were my first real girlfriend. I loved you. You know that, right?"

"I feel the same way. I miss you, Liam. I've always thought about you. We were young and dumb, and we needed to explore the world, but I feel like it's our time now."

She inched her way closer to me and rubbed her foot on my leg under the table. She didn't get what I was saying at all.

I backed off. "I—"

My phone rang. Saved for another minute. "Hello," I said, holding up my pointer finger to Samantha.

"I'm going to the bathroom," she whispered.

I nodded and watched her walk away and out of view. She returned to the table just as I was hanging up my phone.

Who was it this time?" she said, annoyance clearly evident in her voice.

I needed to be more forward, I guess. "Sam, you're right, we were both young when we broke up. I was never myself after my parents died, and I know a big reason we split up is because I cut you out. I was broken and hurt and depressed."

She put her hand on mine and leaned her head close to mine. "I know."

"I had no idea you still had feelings for me. Sure, you were flirty at the fundraiser, but I thought that was just old habits, but a part of me kind of knew you had feelings for me. I should have had this conversation that night."

I needed to find the words to explain what was in my head, but this was new to me. I was never good at opening up to someone else. It had cost me relationships in the past. The only person I could open up to was Vivian. How ironic. The girl who did not want me back.

She nodded at me with a hopeful expression.

"But when I announced how I felt for Vivian at the fundraiser, I meant it. Sure, she turned me down, and she doesn't feel the same way about me as I do her but my feelings have not disappeared."

She looked down and sighed. "I was afraid you were going to say that."

"You're someone I have so much love and respect for and that's why I have to be honest with you."

Her eyes teared up, and her lip quivered. I was so bad at reacting when women were upset and crying. I never knew what to say or do but I had enough respect for her to at least try. "I'm not rejecting you. I promise. Roger never should have said that. I guess he wanted us to get back together but I never mentioned anything to him."

She looked down at the table and kept nodding with a disappointed look.

I smiled at her and wiped away the tear beneath her eye with my thumb. "Samantha, you and I haven't spoken in so many years. We've both grown up, and we aren't the same people we were back then." I pursed my lips and ran my thoughts through my head before I spoke. "I just need some time to think."

She nodded. "Okay."

"Let's go back to being friends, okay?"

She nodded.

With perfect timing, our waitress placed the pizza on the table and dished us up a slice of Chicago Style pepperoni pizza.

I took a bite of the crust, my favorite part of the pizza.

Her face brightened. "You still do that?"

"What?"

"Eat your crust first."

I smiled. "I don't know what you're talking about. It's the only way to eat pizza."

"I hate to break it to you, but no one but you eats pizza that way."

"I think everyone else is just eating it wrong." I took another bite and another until the crust was gone. I put my pizza on the plate and took the cheese and pepperoni off with my fork and ate the bottom of the pizza with the little pizza sauce that was left on there.

"And that," she said with a laugh. "Who eats their cheese and toppings last? I take it back, I don't think I could ever date you."

"You little—" I took my napkin off my lap, scrunched it up, and threw it at her.

She caught it and laughed. "Thanks. You aren't getting that back. You'll have to wipe the grease all over your nice pants now."

A waitress walked past us. "Excuse me," I said. "Can you get me another napkin. I must have misplaced mine."

Samantha shook her head and threw my napkin back at me. "Misplaced it, my ass."

Crisis diverted. Maybe I was getting better at this whole communication thing. But I would not tell her all I could think about was Vivian's ChapStick, the smell of peaches still embedded in my nostrils. I needed to stay away. Far, far away from Vivian or she would ruin me. If she hadn't already.

# CHAPTER 31
## *Vivian*

THAT KISS. The intensity and desperation. The way he pushed me against the wall with a mixture of confidence and aggression. I waved air in my face to cool off. No matter how hard I tried or how busy it got in my bar, the only thing I thought about was Liam and his damn lips.

When Alyssa called out last call, we poured ourselves drinks and watched the last few customers rush to finish their drinks.

"Are you going to talk about it?"

My head snapped her way.

"Oh, come on. I'm dying to hear. Tell me you're giving him a chance. That man has been crushing on you for so long."

I shook my head.

She pulled out her phone. "If you don't tell me I'm going to call him and get details."

I grabbed her phone and held it behind my back. "Oh no you aren't. I'll fire you."

"Okay." She threw a towel on the back counter.

Before she could take another step, I grabbed her arm. "Fine."

Her eyes widened and excitement radiated from her expression. "Spill it."

"Okay, I turned him down."

"What? Why?"

"Honestly? Because I'm scared. I'm scared about the feelings I have for him. I'm scared of letting myself fall in love with him and then he breaks my heart. Breaking me. I don't think I can do it."

She placed her hands on my shoulders to steady me. "First of all, it's okay to be scared. I'm scared and I've been with Scott for a long time. Secondly, Liam would never break your heart. He's so head over heels for you. He'd never risk losing you if you gave him a chance. You have to open up your heart. Take a risk. Let yourself love."

I nodded. I knew she was right, but letting it happen was so hard. I struggled to get him out of my head. I wanted what his parents had but … there were still so many uncertainties. "What if we give it a shot and we're just too opposite and better off as friends? I don't want to lose him. He's my best friend."

"What am I? Chopped liver? C'mon."

"You know what I mean."

"Viv, if you turn him down what will be different? After what I walked in on, it already looks like you've crossed the line. You can't turn back now to being just friends. Maybe someday, but not after you devoured each other's faces. You guys were intense and hot as hell."

"Why am I taking advice from someone who is hardly a day over twenty-one?".

She grabbed my hair and yanked on it with enough force to throw off my balance but not enough to hurt me.

"Hey!" I pulled away from her.

The two men laughed and pointed at us.

"This is hot," one of them said.

The other started catcalling.

"Calm down, we're just messing around," I said and waved the bar towel in the air. "Now finish up those drinks and get the hell out of here. Would you? I've got things to do."

The two guys were regulars and loved to give us crap. They finished their drinks and walked over to the door with a wave.

I went to follow them, but the sound of glass shattering behind me had me turning around. I rushed to Alyssa's side to help her sweep up the glass.

"Thank you. Should I just put it in the garbage?"

I pointed toward the back. "Just dump it in the dumpster out back."

I held the back door for her. "Crap, I didn't lock the front door," I said.

I pulled my keys out of my pocket and sifted through them as I made the last few steps to the front door, not paying any attention to what was in front of me. Just as I found the right key, the door jerked open and threw me off balance.

Cold blue eyes stared at me. "Jimmy? What are you doing here?"

He put his hand out when I tried to close the door on him.

"I need to talk to you."

The hair on the back of my neck stood on end. Liam was not here to save me this time. "Not today, Jimmy. We're closed. You can come back tomorrow, and I'll hear you out."

My heart beat heavy in my chest and my body stiffened. All I could think about was Alyssa. What if he hurt her?

He took a step in my direction, his eyes wide and furious. "Who the hell overbid me on this building?"

I backed up and put my hands out for protection. "I don't know, Jimmy. I really don't know. Please leave."

He kept moving on me.

"You know who bought it. I know you do. Quit lying. Was it your brother?" He shook his head. "How about your parents? I know you could never afford it. Mommy, Daddy, come to my rescue?"

I shook my head. "No. They didn't." I had a feeling my parents must have bought the building. They were the only people I knew who could afford to outbid him.

"You're still running to Mommy and Daddy for help. Aren't you? You can't do anything on your own. I'm surprised you can even run this place by yourself."

His words were mean but the anger behind them was all that concerned me right now. I had to figure out how to get him the hell out of the bar before someone got hurt.

"I really don't know, Jimmy. Just leave, please. I'm tired and I need to go home."

His teeth clenched together, the muscles in his jaw evident. He laughed like an evil Disney villain. "You aren't going anywhere until I get some answers so get comfortable."

I continued to slowly walk backward. When I got close to the bar, he shoved me onto a stool, and he stepped behind the bar. I tried to get up, but he grabbed my arm from across the bar.

He pointed at the bar stool. "Oh, no you don't. Sit."

I was not going to test him. What could I use to protect myself if he got vicious?

"Who else is here with you?"

Should I tell him Liam was here and hope that would scare him away? Tell him no one so he would not go looking for Alyssa? My mind went blank, my heart pounding harder, my hands wet with sweat. "No one is here." I just hoped Alyssa would hear us before she stepped back into view and called the police. I didn't want anything to happen to her.

His grin widened. He looked around as if he was debating whether or not he believed me.

"Why do I think you're lying to me? Is every word that comes out of your mouth a lie now?"

I shook my head. "I'm not lying, but Liam may be

showing up soon to give me a ride home." Hopefully that would scare him. Liam intimidated Jimmy the last time he tried to hurt me. Was he dumb enough to try again when he thought there was a chance Liam could show up?

He walked around the bar, and picked up a bottle of vodka. My hands held on to the bar stool to keep me steady.

He leaned over the bar and grabbed two shot glasses off the bar rail.

"Every time you lie to me you're going to take a shot of vodka." The tone of his voice was threatening and scared me.

"Your car is parked out front so don't lie to me." He poured a shot and pushed it in front of me.

I took the shot.

"Let's try this again. Who bought this fucking building, Viv?"

His voice was deep and intimidating but I would not let him see me flinch or that he was scaring me. "I don't know," I whispered.

He swiped the glass off the bar. The sound of glass shattering as it hit the floor had my stomach in my throat. I flinched when he acted like he was going to hit me with a backhand, but he stopped his arm close to my face and laughed when I flinched. He lifted my chin, and I did not dare move.

He put his thumb to my lip and slowly ran it from side to side, staring into my eyes with a blank expression.

His eyes scanned my body and made me ill. Did I have time to run?

"It was your boyfriend. Wasn't it?"

"What boyfriend?"

I acted as though I had no idea who he was talking about but we both knew.

He pounded his closed fist on the bar, a look of anger building in his expression. "Stop messing with me, Viv."

"I'm not."

"That boyfriend with the big muscles and the empty brain did this. I should have known it was him. He's obsessed with you."

He poured another shot and placed it on the bar in front of me. "Take the shot. Actually, drink the rest of this bottle." He pushed the bottle in front of me.

My hand flew up to catch it before it fell over.

"You want me to drink all of this, a half bottle? I'll puke. No way," I said. I put my hand over the top of the bottle.

"Everything okay in here? I already called 9-1-1."

The sound of Alyssa's voice echoed off the empty walls, but I had a feeling she was bluffing.

He stood up, his eyes still focused on mine. "Well, it sure is your lucky day. Isn't it?" He pointed his finger in my face. "This isn't over."

I struggled to move my feet after he walked away. Alyssa followed him to the door and the minute he stepped outside she slammed the door and locked it. She hurried to my side and hugged me.

"Are you okay? Did he hurt you?"

I shook my head. "What did I ever see in that guy? I'm really messed up. You know that?"

She laughed. "We all make mistakes. You should see some of my exes." Her expression turned serious. "Are you sure you're okay?"

"Yeah. Yeah. I just need to sit down for a few minutes before I leave."

I was scared to leave. What if he was waiting outside for me? Luckily, I'd never taken him to my apartment. Maybe he didn't know where I lived.

"Okay," Alyssa said. I'll clean up this mess and stick around for a little bit. I'm not leaving you alone right now.

# CHAPTER 32

## Liam

I SAT up in bed with my light on and stared at my phone, the kiss on my mind. No woman has ever kissed me that way. The passion and intensity. Why was she trying so hard to fight it?

Just as I was putting my phone on the charger, it rang. Vivian? Why was she calling so late? Was she jealous? Calling to apologize? My mind was racing with thoughts. "Hello? Everything alright?"

"Liam, it's Alyssa. From Zenith," she whispered.

"Alyssa. Hi. Why are you calling from Vivian's phone? Is everything okay?"

"Come to the bar if you can. Jimmy showed up here and… Viv needs you."

I searched the floor for my pants. "Is he still there? I swear I'll kill that guy if he lays another finger on her."

"He's gone and the doors are locked, but she's shook up a bit. He didn't hurt her. But I think she would be a lot better if you gave her a ride home. She has her car here, but I don't think she should drive."

I held the phone against my shoulder while trying to

balance on one foot and pull on my pants. My body was shaking with worry. The phone went flying so I finished pulling up my pants, then dove for the phone. "Sorry about that. I dropped my phone. Just stay with her. I'm on my way."

I broke several speed limits on the way to the bar. Amazing I did not get pulled over. In record time, I pulled up in front of the restaurant. I knocked on the door and Alyssa used the keys to let me in then locked the door behind me.

"Where is she?"

She pointed to the back.

"Thanks for calling, Alyssa. You're a good friend. Do you want me to walk you to your car?"

"No, but can you lock up? My boyfriend just pulled up."

I locked the door behind her and made my way to Vivian's office. I knocked once and walked in. She was lying on the floor, her hands over her face. I raced to her side and kneeled next to her.

Vivian smiled as she sat up. She wrapped her arms around me and tucked her head into my chest.

"Liam. How did you know?"

"Shush," I said, rubbing the back of her head. "I'm here now. It doesn't matter. Everything's going to be okay."

I stood up so I could help her to her feet. She took my hand, a sign of trust.

I kept hold of her waist to make sure she was steady on her feet. She reached out and put her hand on my shoulder.

"What is this? A Disney movie?" she said with a laugh.

I laughed and pushed her curls out of her face and looked into those beautiful eyes. "Let me guess, Aladdin?"

"Yes, I'm impressed. You know your princess movies," she said, trying to steady herself. " Alyssa called you?"

I did not need to answer. She knew.

"I didn't need you to save me, you know."

I raised an eyebrow and grinned. "Good, because I was a little late for that." The guilt nibbled at my heart for not being here to protect her. "I should have been here."

"No. How were you supposed to know? He scared the crap out of me, but I can take care of myself. Look at these muscles." She held up her arm and flexed for me. I squeezed her arm. She was using humor to calm herself down.

"No kidding. Maybe you need to start saving me."

She pushed me playfully. Her smile widened but tears still pooled in the corners of her eyes.

She sniffled. "Thank you for coming."

I took a tissue off her desk and handed it to her.

"Thanks," she said as she dabbed her eyes. "I hope I didn't ruin your date with Samantha."

"It's after two in the morning. You didn't ruin my date."

Relief showed on her face. She was glad the date ended early.

"After that kiss, I'm surprised I even made it out the door," I said. "It really wasn't a date. Samatha and I would never work out."

"I'm sorry," she said. She bit her lip. I lifted her chin up so I could see her face. Her eyes sparkled with need as she stared back at me.

"I have an idea that might get Jimmy to back off," she said. "Let him know he will never get me back."

"Oh really?" I wanted to kiss those lips. Was this the start of something new? Was she finally letting herself feel her emotions for me?

"Yeah."

She dropped her arms and stepped away from me, her hands now on her hips. "I think he tried to buy this building just to control me. He wants me back, but I also know he's scared of you. He called you my boyfriend with the big muscles."

"He called me that?" I worked out a lot but not exactly the way I thought Jimmy would describe me. I was no body builder.

"Feeling flattered?" she said with a laugh. "I really do think he's scared of you, and I think if you and I pretend to date he will back off. I also need to find out who bought my building. Whoever bought it wants to sell it to me. I need to know what this guy's intentions are. I don't want to deal with another situation like this and get screwed over."

Guilt built up in my chest. "How do you know it's a guy?"

"The banker referred to the buyer as a he."

"Oh."

"I have a feeling my brother got my parents to save the bar, and I don't want it to be them. They both have health issues, and they need that money. They've earned that money. I want to buy this bar on my own or it won't be mine. But I have a feeling it was my dad."

I pursed my lips, trying to figure out what to say.

"If they did buy the building, why didn't they talk to me first? I hate when people throw their money around. My parents have been doing it since I was a kid. They could have talked to me, but instead they felt the need to save me. Like they don't have any faith in my ability to handle this on my own."

Was that what I did? No. I had faith in her. I did it because I refused to let Jimmy have control over her. Who knows what he would do if he had that kind of control?

"But what do you think? Would you like to be my fake boyfriend?"

I wanted to be her real boyfriend but if this was all she was offering then how could I pass it up? But I felt like a fraud. Should I tell her I was the one who bought the building? Not yet. She'd be so angry at me and right now she needed my help.

"I'll be your fake boyfriend. Do you think this will work though?"

She shrugged. "I think so. But being my boyfriend also means you can't quit until we get rid of Jimmy."

"I can stick around for a little while longer."

I was sifting through the extensions when Roger walked into my office.

"We need to talk."

I put down my papers and sighed. "What, Rog?"

"I'm sick and tired of handling all the calls from angry customers. You aren't the same person who started this business with me. That person was hard working and used his head. He kept up with his work and was the face of this company. You've been slacking."

I shook my head. "Aren't you being a bit dramatic here?"

He crossed his arms, his nostrils flaring. "I can't keep doing this with you, Liam. It isn't a joke. I'm leaving."

I stood up. "What? No, you're not. This is our business."

"And you aren't doing your job. I'm not going to keep doing this year after year while you chase tail. You're the face of this company. People love you but they're dropping us. We're losing them because you aren't around anymore."

He was right. I couldn't argue. Too many customers pulled their taxes or decided to go elsewhere.

"Tell me I'm wrong. Tell me you'll stop working at that restaurant so we can keep the business accounts."

I stared at him blankly. I could not say that, and the guilt was eating me alive.

"That's what I thought. I spoke with the building manager, and I got us out of our lease. They have a line of people waiting for space to open up here. He said it shouldn't be a problem."

"What? You've got to be kidding me."

He hung his head. "The offices will be listed this afternoon. I'm sorry, Liam."

Before I could reply he was out the door. I stood there in shock. My bank account was empty and my business had officially failed. So why did I feel a sense of relief?

I drove away, anger building in my chest. I needed to take it out on someone, and I knew who that person was. I found his address on a quick google search and pulled up in front of his crappy little house on the west side of Duluth. As luck had it, Jimmy was on his way outside when I pulled up. I charged over to him and pushed him up against his porch. I moved quickly and pinned my forearm to his throat. "I hear you have a problem staying away from my girl."

I pushed my forearm tighter on his neck when he tried to speak. He tried to claw my arm off him, but I was much stronger. "If you ever come near her bar again, I will kill you. You got it?"

He did not answer, nor could he. I let my arm relax a little because I didn't want him to pass out.

"Well?"

Still no answer.

"If that doesn't scare you, I want you to know Lake Superior is so cold at the bottom that bodies don't decompose so they sink right to the bottom. You don't want to die that way, Jimmy. Do you?"

He shook his head.

"You don't want to know how I know that. Vivian and I are together now, and if she mentions you're coming around one more time, I will follow through with my promise. Do you hear me?"

Tears streamed down his face as he coughed. "Yes."

"Good. We have an understanding then?"

"Yes."

I punched him and threw him on the ground and dropped a wad of cash beside him. All the money I had in my wallet. "Get the hell out of here. I never want to see your face again. Understood?"

He nodded.

"Good."

I walked away and I had a feeling that was last we would hear from him.

# CHAPTER 33

## *Vivian*

"YOU'RE FAKE DATING? Seriously? You think that is going to do anything?"

Olivia was not happy about our arrangement, and she was letting me know exactly how she felt. "Viv, you're in love with the guy you're pretending to date. You can't fake date him."

She held up her hands to emphasize fake date with air quotes. "It's going to end horribly. You do know that, right?"

I brushed her off. "I'm not in love with him. You're over-reacting."

"Yes, you are, you're just bullheaded. But you also know he's in love with you and you'll break his heart when you break off the fake relationship, right?"

She was over thinking way too much. "I love you, Livy, but I think you have way too much time on your hands and not enough in person interaction. You should really get out more."

"I'm busting my butt cleaning your house and making dinner and then I go to Mom and Dad's house almost every day to help them take their meds, clean their house, and take them to their doctors' appointments while raising a toddler on my own. Don't tell me I have too much time on my hands."

Her angry tone had me second guessing my words. "I'm sorry. That's not what I meant. I appreciate you and everything you do around here. Really? And helping with mom and dad. None of our siblings have stepped up to the plate so it's pretty much just us left to take care of them. Thank you for what you do. I never want you to think I'm taking advantage of you."

She shook her head. "I'm sorry. I'm just a little emotional. Tim and Lizzy are getting married in two months and all I can think about is seeing Troy again."

I sat down next to her on the couch and put my arm around her. "You still have feelings for him. Don't you?"

"Yeah. I know you said his ex will always come before me even if she's no longer in this world but—"

"Don't listen to me. I don't know what I'm talking about. Really. I was angry and didn't believe in love. I was trying to protect you. I never should have said that. I never should have pressured you to come back to Duluth. I'm sorry. It was selfish."

She looked over at me and shook her head. "No. Moving back here was my decision. Someone needed to help our parents, and it gave me time to think. I was pregnant. I couldn't stay."

"What are you worried about? With seeing Troy?"

"I'm worried he won't feel the same way about me that I feel about him. I haven't even tried to get a hold of him since I left."

"And has he reached out to you?"

She shook her head.

"He's probably giving your relationship time and giving you space, just like you."

"Maybe."

"I think it'll be good for you to see him. Maybe you'll

figure out what you want. He may just be someone that gives you hope but not actually someone you want to spend the rest of your life with."

"Yeah. I guess I won't know until I see him again."

"How about if we bundle Melody and get some ice cream at Love Creamery?"

"I'm in."


We ate our vegan cones inside the building and stared out the window at the people passing by. A snowstorm was predicted, but right now mud and brown grass surrounded the city. Mother Nature was teasing us with one last snowstorm. Enough to make everyone angry.

We stopped at the grocery store on our way home. Super One was packed with people prepping for the big snowstorm coming. Everyone wanted to stock up on food so they could stay home and not have to deal with going outside until it was over. Some people doubted it would hit us and others said it was going to trap us in our home for days.

As for me? I gave it no further thought. Liam and I were the only ones working tonight, along with two cooks and a dishwasher. We all knew it would be a quiet night. Not many people liked to brave the storm when they could order in and sit home all cozy and safe in their houses until the storm was over. Then the restaurant would be full again.

As predicted, the storm produced a heavy whiteout, and business was slow.

I walked behind the corner and Liam looked up from the cooler where he was stocking beer. "Should we close up early tonight since we only have a handful of people in here? Looks like it's getting pretty bad out there." Liam said.

I shook my head. "How about if we are productive instead and do inventory? I already told the kitchen staff to close down."

"I guess we can do that. Did you drive tonight?"

I shook my head. "No. I figured my fake boyfriend could drive me home with his big old truck." I winked at him, and he laughed.

By eleven at night the bar was empty. I peeked out the window." It's really coming down out there."

"I think we should close up now. It's pretty bad," Liam said.

I opened up the front door and peeked outside. "Yeah, I think you're right. Let me get the lights. We can finish up the basement inventory tomorrow."

We trudged through the snow, the bottom of my pants wet and cold, but all I cared about was getting home safely. There had to be a foot of snow already with no sign of it slowing down any time soon.

The roads were slippery, and so far, I counted three cars in the ditch. A car in front of us made its way around a corner and slid into the ditch. Liam hit the brakes. Our car spun out of control and we slid into the ditch, tail end first.

I braced for impact in case we rolled, but we stopped suddenly. No airbags went off. All I could hear was the sound of my heavy breathing.

"Are you okay?" Liam said with a painful grunt.

"I'm okay. Are you?"

He grimaced. "I think I bent my thumb back, but other than that I'm okay."

We climbed out of the truck. Heavy snow continued to fall.

"I'll check on the other car and make sure they're okay," Liam said.

I nodded and followed him. We trudged through the snow rather than risk falling on the slippery roadway. Someone else was likely to come in right behind us.

Liam opened up the car door. "Are you okay? Can you get out?"

Liam moved to the side as a man crawled out of the door.

"Lee?" Liam said. "What are the odds? Did you call the police?"

"Yeah, I called. They're sending a tow truck."

"Why don't you sit in my truck with us? It's safer than standing in the ditch or on the side of the road. Plus, it's really cold."

I recognized the man from the other car, but I could not place him.

We got into the truck. Lee sat in the back.

"Wow, what are the odds you'd be the one to rescue me," Lee said with a laugh.

Liam looked at him and shook his head as if he was trying to get him to stop talking. Why?

"One hell of a deal you made on that building by the way. I can't believe you overbid that sketchy guy and paid in cash."

Liam put his head down. I was even more confused. "You bought a building?"

Liam's face turned white. Why was he so nervous? Then it hit me. "Wait. Did you buy my building?"

"Oh, shit," Lee said from the back seat. "You must be Vivian."

Liam shot me a guilty look. "I'm so sorry, Viv. I can explain."

Now I remember where I saw him. He was the other banker Justin was talking to when Tim and I were there. How could Liam do this to me?

# CHAPTER 34

## *Liam*

THE WAIT for the police and tow truck felt like forever. Vivian would not look at me or talk to me and never had she directed such an angry expression at me. And it hurt. It broke me. Maybe I should have told her. Didn't she understand I was protecting her?

After the tow finally came and Lee apologized over and over, I took her home and she slammed the door without one word. I tried talking to her, explaining what happened but she would not listen, nor did I blame her. But couldn't she see I did it to help her?

Early the next morning I headed to the office before going over to the restaurant. Boxes jammed my office. Roger was not kidding. He was done. But did I really blame him? Everything around me was crumbling, and both problems were my fault. The poor decisions I made put me into this mess. I packed up my stuff and carried the boxes out to my car. All that was left was my computer, files, and desk supplies.

I felt terrible about letting my brother down but if I was honest with myself, our business closing was a relief.

Running a business was a lot of work and took so much time, and my brother and I struggled to see eye to eye. The company had gotten in between our relationship.

As I went to pick up the last box to haul out to my car, I noticed the door to my brother's office was open. I knocked and pushed the door open. Roger's head popped up from papers on his desk.

"I see you've started packing," he said without emotion.

"Yeah. About that. I want to apologize—"

He stood and raised his hand to stop me. "You don't need to apologize. This has never been your dream, Liam. It's mine. I wanted to run this place with you."

"I know. I screwed up."

He took a step toward me. "That's what you aren't getting, brother. I pushed you into this. I knew it wasn't what you wanted, but you're my brother and I wanted to run a business with you more than anyone. I pushed when I knew it wasn't what you wanted."

I had forgotten how many times I turned him down before he finally rented the office space and gave me no choice.

"But to be honest, I wanted to work with you, too. I love seeing you every day and having a business together, but I just can't sit down and work in an office. You know me. My adult ADHD kicks in, and I can't be confined to a desk. I should have told you sooner, but I thought it would work out. I thought I'd get used to it."

"And you fell in love."

My jaw dropped. I couldn't deny it.

"You don't think we can't see the way you look at Vivian? I was jealous. I hated that you were working for her when you should have been here with me. I missed my brother. I even tried to throw Samantha your way, but that didn't work."

"Yeah, thanks for that. You do that again and next time I won't be so nice. Vivian needed me," I said, not fighting his observations. What he was saying was true, but I also hated punching numbers all day.

"And how is that working out for you exactly?"

I chewed on my lip. I hated to admit the truth. "I messed it up."

"What happened?"

"I thought I was doing something to help her, and I just made everything worse and now she knows, and she hates me."

"I highly doubt that. I saw the way she looks at you." He crossed his arms. "Can you fix this?"

"What?"

"Can you fix this. This problem between the two of you?"

I nodded. "I think so." My eyes welled with tears, but I blinked them away.

"Then fix it, brother. I'm sorry I didn't listen to you, and I'm sorry I've been a jerk."

I took another step to close the gap between us and wrapped my arms around him, patting his back in a manly, brotherly hug.

We held on for longer than I expected.

Roger was the first one to back off. "Okay, no crying on my suit, okay? I just got this thing dry-cleaned."

I laughed. "We good?"

"Better than good," he said. "Now go get your girlfriend."

I nodded and off to the bar I went.

I swept and mopped the floor after finishing the inventory. Vivian arrived around noon. She tried to walk past me, her heels echoing off the walls and wooden floor.

"Vivian."

She turned around, an angry glimmer in her eyes. To say that glare did not break my heart and make me want to hide behind the bar would be a lie. "Can I talk to you?"

"I have a lot to do," she said.

"Please. Just give me five minutes."

She looked at her watch and tapped it. "Fine. Let's go into my office."

I followed her into her office and shut the door behind me.

She crossed her arms and stood behind her desk, staring at me in an intimidating way.

I cleared my throat, unsure how to start. "First off, I want to tell you how sorry I am for not telling you."

She stared at me with a brooding look on her face. "Sorry for not telling me or sorry for getting caught?"

She would not let me off easy. "Okay, I deserved that."

"Were you ever going to tell me?"

I wiped the sweat off my brow. "When I found out Jimmy was trying to buy the building and take over the bar, it left me no choice. I had to do something. I went to the bank, and I overbid because the truth is, this building is worth a lot. It was worth the investment."

She rolled her eyes. "You're lying again."

No, the building was worth the investment. She was worth the investment. Her brown curls were distracting. I wanted to wrap my fingers around the curl hanging over her eyes. I wanted to smell her, hold her, kiss her. But I'd be lucky if she even spoke to me again.

I cleared my throat again. I needed to be careful how I worded this or I could lose her forever. "I wanted to tell you, but I knew you'd turn me down. I know you, and I knew you would think it was charity even though that was the furthest from the truth."

"How do you know that when you never asked me?"

"Would you have turned it down?"

She looked away. She knew as well as I did, she would have thought my offer was charity. She never would have allowed me to do it without a fight. "Listen, I know what I did. The way I went about it was wrong. But I love your restaurant. I love it more than I ever thought I would."

She just stared at me blankly.

"You're my best friend, and I know you better than anyone else."

"You can't just buy the building my restaurant is in, Liam. That isn't what friends do without even asking my opinion. I know you thought you were doing something nice, but you knew how upset I felt when I thought my brother and my parents bought it. And you never said a word."

I nodded. She was right. I did know and that made me hide it more. "I didn't want you to lose your restaurant."

I took a step toward her, and she didn't step back.

"Why do you even care? You put in your two weeks."

"Are you kidding me? This is my home. I'm here more than I'm at my own business."

"But it caused you to fall behind, Liam. It's obvious you need to spend more time at your real workplace."

I ran my fingers through my hair. I needed to tell her. "Roger and I no longer have a business."

Her angry face changed into a look of shock. "What? Why?"

"Because this is where I belong, Viv. Don't you see that? I belong here with you."

She deadpanned. "You need to go, Liam. Talk to your brother and save your business." She turned her back to me and when I tried to approach her, she waved me away. "Go!"

"Okay, okay. I'm sorry."

I wanted to stay but that would only piss her off more. She needed time so I would give her time.

# CHAPTER 35
## *Vivian*

ONCE THE DOOR shut behind him, I broke down and slid to the floor. Damn him. How dare he go behind my back and purchase this building and my bar from underneath me? He was just as bad as my family. Nor did he bother to deny it when I accused him.

How could he be so stupid to get rid of his business? I knew it was because I needed him, and he always jumped at the chance to help me out. I put pressure on him to work so many hours during tax season that his schedule interfered with his business. I felt terrible. He quit or lost his job because of me.

I picked up my phone and called the only person who I trusted to talk me through this right now.

"Viv, everything okay?" Tim seemed surprised to hear from me.

The tears had yet to stop. I tried to talk but my nasally voice gave me away.

"No, I'm not okay. Tell me you didn't know about Liam. Tell me you didn't know he bought my building."

The line went silent.

"You knew?"

I needed to hear it from him. He hardly knew Liam. Why would my brother keep this from me?

"Viv, listen, you never would have let him buy the building if I had told you. He cleared out his savings. He had to protect you from Jimmy."

My chest burned. "He emptied his savings?"

"I thought you knew. He paid in cash. What did he tell you?"

"He finally admitted he bought the building but he never told me he emptied his savings."

He sighed. "You know he loves you, right? He sacrificed everything because he loves you and he believes in you. Don't be so hard on him."

How could he blame this mess on me? "How long have you known, Tim? How long did you know what he was doing? Did you plan this, too?"

"No, Viv. Although if he would have asked me first, I would have supported him, I'm not going to lie. He sacrificed everything for you, and he is willing to sell your restaurant back to you even though he lost everything. That is pretty selfless. Maybe you need to think this over before you write him off and decide he did this to be a jerk."

Too late. But Tim had a point, and I hated it when my brother was right. "I hate when you're right."

He laughed. "He's a keeper, Viv. He's a keeper."

Time to swallow my pride and come up with a plan I could live with.

"Next weekend is our bridal shower at Riverside. Please tell me you'll come."

"I wouldn't miss it for the world," I said.

"I'm calling Liv next to remind her. Could you also invite Liam?"

"Really, Tim? Right now you ask me this? Why don't you call him yourself since the two of you are buddy-buddy now."

"Still the same old Viv. I would expect nothing less. I'll call him, too."

I hung up without saying good-bye. Why did he always have to be right?

Phoning Liam would not work. I needed to speak to him in person. His truck was out front when I pulled up.

I knocked on the front door and waited. A couple minutes went by and no Liam. I turned away to leave when he opened the door with wet hair and a towel around his waist.

"Of course, I show up and you're naked."

He looked at me sideways as I pushed right past him and into his home.

"Come on in," he said with a laugh. "I'll get some clothes on."

Good. If he stood there in a towel and nothing else, I would never be able to have this talk. His body did something to my brain, and I forgot for a moment the reason I was even here.

He came back wearing a Duluth Bulldogs sweatshirt and gray sweatpants. Who looked that good when they were dressed in lounge clothes?

"Listen, I've been thinking a lot about what you did. First of all, don't ever again go behind my back and get my brother involved in your scheming."

He looked away, not even denying it.

"Secondly, I want to come up with a new contract."

He looked at me, an eyebrow raised.

"Do you plan on staying at my bar?"

"I'd like to. If you'll have me."

"Then I have a proposal for you. How about we run the bar together? Fifty-fifty?"

Still the raised eyebrow. "Really? You want to be partners?"

"Well, I get final say, but yes. Right now, the bar is yours as much as it's mine. And now that you have extra time on your hands, it's only right."

I took a step toward him and pulled on his sweatshirt strings, tracing the bulldog on the front of it.

"Hmm, I guess I'll need to think about it."

His eyes told me he had nothing to think about. He was just messing with me. I leaned in closer. "I also think you need to make it up to me by taking me to dinner."

"Oh, really?" His hand rested on my jaw, his thumb rubbing my cheek. Goosebumps rose on my arms.

"Really."

"I may be able to free up my busy calendar."

I smiled and a hot blush rose up my cheeks. I was his only plans right now. I liked that.

"Vivian, are you asking me out on a date?"

I leaned closer, just a whisper away. Our eyes locked. "I wouldn't dare."

I walked out the door. He needed to have some sort of punishment for what he did, and I think he had finally learned his lesson.

# CHAPTER 36

## Liam

I'M NOT sure how long I stared at my front door after she walked out. Did she just ask me on a date or was I dreaming?

I decided to change the plans and cook for her. I wanted to showcase my skills and show her what else I could add to the restaurant. I had to impress her. I grilled a couple fillet mignons and prepared twice baked potatoes, my mother's famous coleslaw, and strawberry shortcake for dessert.

She showed up wearing tight jeans and a fitted pink sweater that dipped around her collarbone. Gorgeous.

To say I impressed her with my cooking would be an understatement.

"Liam, this steak is amazing. You need to add it to the menu. I've been thinking about the future of the restaurant. We should take out a couple items on the menu that don't sell as well and add some steak and a couple other dishes. This coleslaw is chef's kiss. How did you learn to cook like this?"

I smiled, loving the way the compliments flowed out of her mouth. I'd never had anyone I wanted to cook for other than my own parents. I liked to cook but I never made time to until now.

"My mother."

She blushed. "Sounds like your mother did a fine job of raising you."

"Oh really."

Now she blushed. "Listen, it's my turn to apologize to you."

I shook my head, but she put her hand on mine to stop me.

I let out a humorous laugh, then dragged my hand through my hair. "I'm all ears."

"I know I've been a jerk." Her voice cracked slightly. "I've been fighting the feelings I've had for you longer than I realized."

I sat back in my chair, thoroughly enjoying this moment. I'd waited a long time for this.

She leaned closer, just enough that it made my breath catch. "I never wanted to believe in love. The fundraiser, the bar, giving up your business. Everything you've done, you've done for me. For your love for the bar."

I swallowed. "Viv…"

"Let me finish. I'm in love with you, Liam. You were right."

I loved to hear those words coming out of her mouth. If only I could rewind them and hear them again. I dared not ask her to repeat them for fear she would take it all back. I sat there quietly, letting her speak.

"I thought I could step away. That I'd stop feeling this way." Her words came out rough, like they had been clawing their way out for months. "I'm done pretending my feelings aren't mutual just because I'm scared.."

Silenced filled the small space between us, the room thick and heavy.

My heart slammed against my ribs. Panic and something hotter tingled in my chest. I don't know what I would do if she changed her mind again.

She looked at me, waiting for me to reply.

"Well? What do you—"

"Oh, wow." I cut in quietly. "I know you didn't think you would ever believe in love and then you met my parents but even when you saw love right before your eyes you told me you did not believe it was out there for you. Love isn't just for some people. Everyone can find love when they open up their hearts and their minds. I want nothing more than to be with you, but I worry you will change your mind again, and I'm not sure I can endure this all over again."

She took a sip of wine, then looked into my eyes. She moved closer, her mouth now so close to mine.

My hands found their way to her face. Our kiss turned deeper than the last time, hungrier. She pulled away.

"This isn't safe. This isn't controlled. This is everything I've been trying to avoid. But for once I'm not afraid. You're worth the risk, Liam."

I rested my forehead against hers, my voice low and wrecked. "I'm all in, Vivian. I'm just glad you finally see what I've seen all along."

I picked her up off the chair and carried her like a bride into my bedroom, where she belonged. In bed right next to me. The world was finally right.

I laid her down on my bed and crawled on top of her, finally curling my finger around her beautiful brunette curls. "Vivian, will you go to your brother's engagement party with me?"

"I would love to. Now kiss me."

I praised her body inch by inch with my kisses and then my tongue and finally we made love well into the night. We rolled around in my bedsheets for hours, our hearts connecting at another level. She was perfect. She was Vivian, and now she was mine.

# CHAPTER 37

## *Vivian*

"I CAN'T BELIEVE the two of you are finally together. I hate to say I told you so, but I told you so," Olivia said.

"Yeah, yeah, yeah. Now, how do you feel about seeing Troy again?"

"I'm okay."

My sister looked everything but okay.

"I'm just glad we're staying at Pine Beach in a cabin. I love Pine Beach. It's so beautiful there. It's going to be sixty degrees so we may not be able to go boating just yet, but we can kayak while we're there."

I laughed. "You and your kayaking."

We grabbed our bags and Olivia picked up Melody. "Is he waiting outside?"

As if on cue, there was a knock on our door. I opened the door and Liam's lips quickly met mine as I dropped the suitcases to jump into his arms.

"Oh, get a room," Olivia said, but her smile gave away how much she enjoyed seeing us together.

He kissed me one last time, then bent down to pick up my stuff.

"Are you ladies ready?"

We both nodded and followed him outside. Once Olivia and Melody were in the car, he shut the door.

"Wait," I said before he could open his door.

He walked back to me, standing by the back door of his truck.

"Open your hand."

He did as I said, and I dropped my keys to the restaurant into his hand. "It's official. It's now our restaurant."

He smiled. "I have something for you, too." He reached into his pocket and placed a key in my hand.

I gave him a confused look.

"This is me giving you the key to my house and the key to my heart."

I forgot how to breathe.

"Breathe, Viv," he said, as if he could read my mind. "If you aren't ready to move in with me that's okay."

"It's just a big step for me."

He grabbed my hand and pulled me in for a kiss. "I know it is. Take your time. Let that key sit in your pocket for the week while we're in Side Lake. You can give me an answer when we get back."

He got me. He truly got me. He'd love me no matter what and that helped me relax. I stepped on my tippy toes to reach his lips again. "This is why I love you. Thank you."

I put the key in my pocket and made my way to the passenger side door.

"Are you ready to meet Olivia and Tim's Side Lake friends?"

"Absolutely."

He looked into the rear-view mirror and adjusted it so he could see Olivia.

"Are you ready, Liv?"

"It's too late to turn back now," she said.

Melody had already fallen asleep in her car seat, and she

remained asleep until we pulled up at Pine Beach Resort, close to two hours later.

Liam got out first and opened the door for Olivia. My mother stood out front of the beautiful newly remodeled cabin at Pine Beach. My father sat on the chair on the deck. Their health problems were really starting to show, and I wondered if Dad should be driving. Olivia usually drove them both to their medical appointments, but dad insisted on driving them up north. I was surprised they actually found the place.

"You know Mary Higgins Clark is rumored to have stayed in this cabin and written some of her books here," my mother said.

She was a huge fan of Mary Higgins Clark.

"I did not know that," I said, taking Melody out of her car seat. "Mom, you remember Liam from the fundraiser."

My mother hugged him. "I sure do. Any man who can steal this girl's heart is a man I'd like to get to know better. She's a stubborn one," she said with a laugh.

"Mom," I said in warning.

Liam laughed because we both knew my mother knew me well.

We brought everything inside and unpacked.

"We're leaving for a barbecue and bonfire at the house of one of Lizzy and Tim's friends. You guys ready?"

Olivia turned pale but nodded without another word.

I patted her shoulder before slipping into the front seat. Olivia was nervous. I was partly guilty for taking her away from this place. Away from Troy. But now I was ready to help her fix it.

*Sneak Peek*

Book 2 in the Admonson Sisters Series
Meet Me in Side Lake
Coming August, 2026

*Olivia*

I LOOKED out my window to catch the green sign, Turtle Creek Road. My lungs deflated. Would Troy even speak to me? Look at me? Would it be weird? Too much time had passed since we last spoke.

We pulled into Ethan and Kat's driveway. I'd turned down staying at their bed and breakfast as soon as Tim mentioned it. I told him we would be more comfortable in a cabin with the baby and everything. He didn't ask any questions, but I was pretty sure I heard Lizzy whispering to him in the background. She knew. Troy was, in fact, her uncle and like a father to her. We made our way around to the gazebo looking over the lake. The ice had finally melted, and the lake was a dark blue. May's spring weather brought hope that summer would soon be on its way.

The memories came flooding back as I stared out at West Sturgeon Lake. The waves crashed against the shore and the smell of the bonfire brought me back to last summer. The laughs, the friendship, the days spent on the lake and in the sun.

My mother stole Melody from me right after the introductions were made. Seeing all my friends again was so great.

Kat, Ethan, Maddy, Brad, Lyndsey, Kevin, and their kids all met us outside.

I snuck away and made my way down the stairs to get a glimpse of the lake to calm my nerves before I saw Troy. My hands were shaking. The air was cold and wet. I closed my eyes and listened to the sound of the lake and smiled.

I heard the familiar sound of paws descending the stairs behind me. I dropped to my knees as Hope came running at me at full speed. I knew better than to stand when Hope got excited. Last time I ended up in the water. She jumped into my arms and licked my face. Her warmth brightened my mood. I hugged her tight and scratched around her soft face.

"I missed you too, Hope." She panted in my face, her long tongue hanging out of her mouth, and she licked my cheek again. I giggled.

"Well, look who it is."

I jerked my head to see Troy standing behind me. Was he even more handsome than the last time I saw him? Had he been lifting weights and working out? I stared, my heart and brain checking him out.

"I met your daughter up there," he said, completely skipping the small talk.

"Melody?" I said as if there could be another daughter up there that he was talking about. My words embarrassed me.

He took another step closer.

I looked down, too anxious to look him directly in the eyes. "Yeah, she's almost seven months old already."

"Has it really been that long?" His eyes stared into mine so deeply I had to look away.

I saw a woman with blond hair walk down the stairs behind him. I squinted to see if it was someone I knew, but I'd never seen her before.

"Troy, I was wondering where you disappeared to."

His cheeks turned red, and I was sure it was not from the chilly air.

He cleared his throat. "Liv, meet Indigo. Indigo, Olivia."

I walked over and shook her hand. She responded, then stepped closer to Troy. Territorial.

"The burgers are ready if you guys are getting hungry. Nice to meet you, Olivia," she said. She looked over at Troy and nodded. He nodded back, and we both watched her disappear up the steps. She was beautiful and tiny and everything I was not.

I swallowed. What do I even say to him? Was that your girlfriend? I wanted to give him some snarky comment, so he felt as broken as me at seeing them have their own silent language. I took a step back and put my foot right into a mud puddle, sending me toppling to the ground.

Troy jumped to catch me in his arms as I fell. Hope yelped like watching me fall worried her.

I wished the lake would open up and swallow me whole. This was going to be a long week. The pain in my foot was throbbing.

Troy helped me as I tried to stand up, but I lost my balance as soon as I put any weight on it.

"Why don't we get you into that chair," he said, nodding toward the lawn chair just a few feet away. I had no choice but to put my arm around his neck as I hopped on one foot with his support and sat down.

He kneeled in front of me, and I stared at him as he took off my shoe and sock to examine my foot. It's funny how Troy kneeling before me made the excruciating pain in my foot go away.

"Point your foot," he said.

I did as he asked. He held onto my ankle. "Can you move your foot? Draw air circles."

I focused on moving my foot and ankle, doing as he instructed. "Yeah. It hurts but I don't think it's broken."

He nodded, digging his fingers into my ankle and massaging it. His touch made me weak, and my heart fluttered in response. He put down my foot and pulled the phone out of his pocket to make a phone call.

Five minutes later, Tim was running down the stairs with Lizzy following close behind with an ice pack in her hand.

Troy put another chair in front of me and guided my foot to the armrest. "Set your foot right here so we can elevate it."

He grabbed the towel and icepack from Lizzy and wrapped the icepack up and placed it on my ankle. I was not ready for it and the cold made me wince.

"It's okay. It'll help," Troy said. His scruffy face and strong jaw up close had me dreaming about what it would feel like to reach out and touch it. His skin was tan but soft and smooth as if he always wore sunblock. The wrinkles around the corner of his eyes made him look mature and handsome. I missed looking at his face. My lips touching those soft lips.

Troy was the best Novocain I could ask for.

"Are you okay?" Tim said, kneeling next to Troy.

I wanted to tell him to go away and let me be, but what Troy and I had was short lived. He had a new girlfriend now.

"You're here for five minutes, and you're already hurt," Tim said with a smirk.

"She can move it, so I think she just rolled it. Do you want to go to the hospital or have Kevin take a look? He's a first responder," Troy said.

I forgot Kevin was a police officer. It made sense he had to have training for instances like this.

I smiled. "Kevin can take a look at it but let's go up by the house. It's a bit chilly down here and I want to sit by the fire."

"Okay," Tim said.

Troy and Tim stood on each side of me and had me hang my arm around their necks while they brought me to my feet. Lizzy grabbed the ice pack and followed us. I put a little weight on my ankle and did not hurt too much, so I slowly walked with minimal weight on my foot.

"You okay?" Troy said, his eyes staring into mine from the side.

I nodded. "Yeah. It doesn't hurt as much as it did at first."

"Good," he said. "Let me lift you up these stairs."

He didn't wait for me to answer and instead picked me up like a bride and carried me up the stairs. I laughed. I never expected the first thirty minutes of my time in Side Lake to be getting injured and rescued by the man I spent the last nine months thinking and dreaming about. Luckily, he could not read my mind.

Had he thought about me at all?

Was he happy with this Indigo? She was model beautiful. It didn't matter. It was really none of my business.

I leaned close to his ear and whispered. "You should probably hand me over to my brother or Indigo might get upset, and I don't need any trouble."

His eyebrows raised in confusion before Tim swooped in.

"Let me grab her," Tim said.

I'm sure he also wanted to avoid the drama. Why didn't he tell me Troy was dating someone?

Tim set me down by the fire and I stood up to try to put weight on my ankle. It hurt a little bit but the more steps I took, the more it loosened up.

"I think I just bruised it. It doesn't really hurt anymore."

Kevin pointed to the chair, and I sat down while he examined my ankle and moved it around. "I think you're right. If it starts hurting again when you're walking, you might want to go in."

I hardly heard a word he was saying as I stared over at Indigo.

Lizzy sat down next to me and Hope jumped up on my lap and put her paws on my shoulders as I hugged her back.

"I think someone is happy you're back," Lizzy said with a smile. "Now that you're here, I can finally ask you. Will you be my maid of honor?"

My eyes filled with tears. "Really? Me?"

She shook her head. "Of course, you. You're my person, Olivia."

Maybe this week would not be as bad as I thought.

Tim took a step closer to us. "And Troy is going to be my best man. Aren't you, buddy?"

I looked over at Troy, sitting across from the fire, his eyes on me. I looked away, unable to get enough air in my lungs. Of course he was the best man. Just my luck. No way was I going to let my feelings for him ruin this wedding for me. He was happy now and that was what mattered. Even if it wasn't with me.

# Acknowledgments

Thank you first of all to my readers. Without your love and support I would not be able to do what I do. You guys are truly amazing.

Thank you to the professionals who made this book possible, my editor Shirley Fedorak, my proofreaders, and Kristin Bryant, my amazing cover designer.

Always a special thanks to my husband, Owen, and daughter Alexis for always listening to my crazy fictional ideas and spending endless hours helping me make this book what it is. Your love and support mean everything to me.

Thank you to my local community for continuing to support me and making me feel special. There is nothing better than being stopped by a stranger who has been touched by one of my stories. It is truly the best feeling in the world.

Lastly, thank you to my friends and family and the teachers who believed in me and pushed me to continue writing when I was young and lacked the confidence to stand on my own. The influence of my past teachers has guided me through all these years of writing and publishing. A good teacher is someone you never forget, and I have so many who have influenced me over the years.

I also want to give a shout out to my sister, Jackie. My whole life you have been the person I have always looked up to and took advice from. Thank you for being the best friend and sister a girl could ever ask for without judgement. You are one of the strongest people I know, and the bravest. I love you.

There is nothing more important to help an author's career than to write a review and spread the word. Thank you, readers, for all you do.

To follow me on social media, I am on Facebook, TikTok, and Instagram. Follow me @JenniferWaltersAuthor

Check out my webpage at JenniferWaltersAuthor.com to sign up for my newsletter and upcoming book signings and releases.